"So, you mean to tell me we're going on a scavenger hunt, following clues set out by a killer?"

Bridget knew her voice had accelerated several octaves, but she didn't care. "How can we be sure Lovelorn won't be hiding somewhere waiting to jump us?"

"We can't. But I don't think he would have gone to so much trouble to plan a scavenger hunt if he didn't intend for us to reach the end. He wants us to play this his way, and he isn't likely to stop the game until we reach the goal."

Who was she kidding? She'd known she was going on this scavenger hunt from the moment she stepped out of the ambulance, allowing her brother to be sprinted off to the hospital without her.

All she could do now was pray she could outsmart the madman who'd decided to use her as a pawn in his real-life game of chance. Last time, she had been attacked without warning. This time, she'd be on guard, and she would not go down without a fight.

Rhonda Starnes is a retired middle school language arts teacher who dreamed of being a published author from the time she was in seventh grade and wrote her first short story. She lives in North Alabama with her husband, who she lovingly refers to as Mountain Man. They enjoy traveling and spending time with their children and grandchildren. Rhonda writes heart-and-soul suspense with rugged heroes and feisty heroines.

Books by Rhonda Starnes

Love Inspired Suspense

Rocky Mountain Revenge
Perilous Wilderness Escape
Tracked Through the Mountains

Visit the Author Profile page at LoveInspired.com.

TRACKED THROUGH THE MOUNTAINS

RHONDA STARNES

LOVE INSPIRED SUSPENSE

INSPIRATIONAL ROMANCE

LOVE INSPIRED® SUSPENSE
INSPIRATIONAL ROMANCE

ISBN-13: 978-1-335-58802-9

PLEASE RECYCLE
THIS PRODUCT IS RECYCLABLE

Recycling programs for this product may not exist in your area.

Tracked Through the Mountains

For questions and comments about the quality of this book, please contact us at CustomerService@Harlequin.com.

Love Inspired
22 Adelaide St. West, 41st Floor
Toronto, Ontario M5H 4E3, Canada
www.LoveInspired.com

Printed in U.S.A.

Trust in the Lord with all thine heart;
and lean not unto thine own understanding. In all
thy ways acknowledge him, and he shall direct thy paths.
—*Proverbs* 3:5-6

For my husband, who has always dreamed of
hiking the Appalachian Trail from Georgia to Maine,
but who put his dream on hold to raise a family.
I love you, Mountain Man!

Also, special thanks to:

Daniel Dixon,
for sharing his experience hiking the AT
and giving me insight into some of the hardships
he faced along the way.

Terri Reed, for your encouragement and support
when I first started writing this story many years ago.

Dina Davis, who saw the potential in this story
when I first entered it into the Blurb to Book pitch
contest in 2015. The feedback you gave me on this story
was much appreciated.

My editor, Tina James, for buying this story
that is near and dear to my heart.

ONE

Sawyer Eldridge maneuvered the John Deere Gator UTV over the uneven, rocky landscape that covered the remote section of Mountain Shadow Ranch that nestled against the foothills of the Great Smoky Mountains. In the ten months that he'd worked as the foreman on Frank and Marie Vincent's ranch, he had come to appreciate the beauty and solitude of this section of land.

He slid a sideways glance at Bridget Vincent, who sat silently in the passenger seat, her posture rigid. This was the first time he could recall the auburn-haired beauty going deep into the woods since her arrival at her grandparents' ranch two months ago to heal from injuries sustained in an attack. He didn't know all the details, but he knew she went to physical therapy twice weekly. "You know, I could have checked the game cameras alone."

"No way. I promised Granddad I'd do my part while he's away."

"You've definitely kept your word. I'd still be working to repair that section of fence near the hayfield if you hadn't helped."

"I'm still surprised Granddad and Grams went on vacation the week before Thanksgiving." She sighed. "I guess, when you own a ranch, there's never a perfect time to take a vacation."

"You're probably right, but I'd say this was as good a time as any. Besides, they'll be back late tomorrow night, which gives them a few days to prepare for all the family arriving for the Thanksgiving weekend." He glanced at her again, noting her pink windburned cheeks, and sighed. "I really should have dropped you off at the farmhouse. If it wasn't so late in the day, I'd turn around now and take you back before checking the game cameras."

As if to emphasize his words, the sun dipped lower in the sky, its pink and orange hues mingling with the shadows on the mountains.

"I appreciate the thought, but Granddad wouldn't approve."

Sawyer couldn't argue with that. One of Frank's hard-and-fast rules was for no one to venture into the area of the ranch referred to as the *back forty* alone. He smiled. The back forty was actually closer to four hundred acres, at the far corner of the property in a valley beyond a creek that flowed from a waterfall on the side of the mountain bordering the twenty-four-hundred-acre ranch. In Sawyer's opinion, it was the most beautiful section of the ranch, full of deer and other wild game. However, with poor cell reception, if someone were to be injured while working in that section of the property, they could easily die before being found. Hence Frank's rule.

A coyote howled in the distance. Bridget twisted in her seat, craning her neck to search the woods. She seemed on edge, and he didn't think her agitation was simply because she heard a wild animal. Did her aversion to being in the woods have anything to do with the accident that sent her all the way from Colorado to Tennessee to recover?

His boss's granddaughter had secrets she wanted to keep hidden. And Sawyer knew all about secrets. In a few months, he'd have to decide if he was going to return to his old life with the FBI or put that career behind him, permanently, and continue working as a ranch foreman. For the time being, Sawyer was content where he was and didn't want to think about the choices he needed to make.

As they approached the ridge that rimmed the back forty, Sawyer slowed the vehicle and switched into four-wheel drive low to give the tires more traction. "Hang on. The ride's bumpy from this point on."

"Um, 'kay," Bridget murmured, as she continued to survey the surrounding area.

He reached across and touched her shoulder. "You need to turn around. It isn't safe to ride like that going down the side of the mountain. Make sure your seat belt is tight."

She looked like she might argue, but then turned and settled in the seat correctly. "Better?"

"Yes. Thank you." He bit back the grin that threatened. Bridget had an independent streak that rivaled any he'd ever seen. He imagined her stubbornness and independence were why she was doing so well after her accident, physically and emotionally. She covered it well, but he had witnessed mild symptoms of post-traumatic stress disorder when she'd arrived at the ranch to rest and recover. Recently, her symptoms were hardly noticeable. Though he had no proof, he suspected the biweekly trips to town involved more than physical therapy for her shoulder and included regular sessions with a counselor.

Many things about her intrigued him, and

had ever since the first time he met her ten months ago and learned that she worked as a bodyguard for her older brother's security firm. He just hoped he had enough time to figure out more about Bridget before she headed home to Colorado in a week.

The ride was indeed bumpy, but they made it to the bottom of the mountain with relative ease. Sawyer quickly located the first two cameras and switched out the SD cards. Then, he headed the Gator across the creek that flowed through the hollow. The last camera was near the edge of the property.

Less than a hundred yards from their destination, Bridget grabbed his arm.

"There's a man. Look." She pointed. "He's running along the fence line."

Slowing the vehicle, Sawyer craned his neck. "Where? I don't see anyone."

"He was sitting on the corner post in front of that large pine. He dropped to the other side of the fence when we crossed the creek."

"It could be one of the ranch hands from Stone Bridge Farm, out fixing fences like we were earlier. But, let's check to be sure." He turned the vehicle in the direction she pointed.

Ping!

A bullet hit the front fender of the UTV.

Sawyer's training kicked in. He pushed Bridget's head down and yanked the wheel toward a large oak tree. Their vehicle offered little protection. If he could get behind the tree, they'd have more cover.

Bridget jerked free of his hold and raised her head, a gun in her hand. She must have worn an ankle holster. She reached to unfasten her seat belt as Sawyer swung the vehicle behind the old oak. He'd barely touched the brake when she opened her door and dived behind the tree.

Sawyer grabbed the shotgun out of the bed of the UTV before he climbed across the seat and joined Bridget on the ground. "How good a look did you get at this guy?"

"Not a good enough one to ID him in a lineup. He was sitting on top of the fence post, a baseball cap pulled low over his face. I couldn't tell if he was trying to get onto our property or leaving it. He dropped to the other side of the fence and ran toward the cluster of trees."

Bridget leaned around the tree and shot in the direction of the property line. Their attacker returned fire and bark rained down as a bullet struck the trunk. Sawyer pulled her back behind the tree, his heart hammering against his ribs. "Don't poke your head out when someone is shooting at you."

"Well, I don't intend to sit here and wait for him to shoot me."

"I agree, but you don't need to go off half-cocked and make yourself an easy target."

Fire lit her eyes. He suspected, if pushed, she had the temper to go with her red hair.

"In case you've forgotten, I'm a trained bodyguard. I know how to take out an assailant."

So do I, he wanted to shout. After all, until eighteen months ago, he'd been on the fast track to become a top-notch profiler for the FBI. Well, until that last case, the one that would forever plague his dreams. Now, he required a full day of hard physical labor to help him sleep at night.

"I need to get closer," Bridget continued, pointing to the tree ten feet to their left, where the game camera was located. "If I can get behind that tree over there, I should be able—"

"Exactly what I was thinking. Only, I'm the one who's going to move closer. Stay put. Draw his fire away from me." Sawyer didn't wait for her agreement. Instead, he bent low to the ground and ran.

A loud pop filled the air, and a bullet struck the front tire of the Gator mere seconds after he passed it. A second shot followed quickly, hitting the ground as he scooted behind the tree trunk. Sawyer met Bridget's eyes and nodded. Then he draped the shotgun sling across his shoulder, grabbed a low-hanging limb and swung into the tree. Adrenaline surged through his veins. Sawyer had to stop this person before he succeeded in his mission to kill them.

Bridget shot in rapid succession in the direction the gunfire had come from, drawing the gunman's attention away from him. Squeezing behind the largest branch, he lifted the shotgun to his shoulder and peered down the barrel. *Okay, creep, where are you?* There. He saw a flash mere seconds before a bullet hit the tree, not three feet below where he stood.

"That's it, buddy," he muttered under his breath. Pulling the trigger, he sent buckshot into the stand of trees.

An engine rumbled to life, and a camouflage-colored ATV sped away from the fence that lined the adjoining property. Sawyer and Bridget continued to shoot, but the driver zigzagged in and out of the trees, adding to the difficulty of hitting a moving target, and soon disappeared from sight.

Sawyer climbed out of the tree. Thankfully,

the bullet had hit a few inches above the game camera, and the SD card was intact.

By the time he got back to the oak tree, Bridget was in the middle of changing the tire, muttering under her breath.

"Need a hand?"

She shook her head, took a deep breath and puffed it out. "No. Thanks. I can do it."

"You know, you don't always have to be so independent." He held out his hand. "Hold on to this. I'll finish changing the tire."

"What is it?"

"The SD card from the game camera. Maybe we can get a better look at our shooter."

She examined the SD card before slipping it into her pocket. "Great. We need to hurry so we can get this to the sheriff."

They both reached for the lug wrench.

"Let me do it." He held firm to the tool.

She looked like she was about to argue, but relinquished her hold without a word. Maybe she realized not everything he did was a strike against her independence.

He finished changing the tire just as the last rays of sunlight disappeared and darkness descended upon them.

Bridget settled into the passenger seat and wrapped her arms around her midsection as if she were cold. "I have a feeling this won't be the last we see of our shooter."

Me, too. Sawyer just hoped the pictures would clue them in on the guy's identity and who or what he was really after.

"Are you sure we shouldn't take the SD card straight to the sheriff?" Bridget asked as she settled into the leather chair in front of her grandfather's desk.

"We don't even know if we got a photo of the guy." Sawyer dragged a chair closer and sat beside her. "If we didn't, there's nothing to turn over to the authorities."

That made sense. She inserted the card into the computer. And shivered as the image of a jet-black coyote loomed on the screen. There had been a time when coming across a wild animal in the woods would have been her biggest fear. Now, she knew two-legged predators could be much more dangerous.

"Wow." Sawyer leaned over Bridget's shoulder and examined the photo. "Black coyotes are rare. Most people never get to see one."

"Yeah, well, I'll have to come back to him later and appreciate his beauty. Right now, I'd rather see if we caught the shooter on camera."

"Of course." He nodded agreement. "Let's reverse the order of the images and jump to the most recent ones."

Sawyer reached for the mouse, his hand closing over hers before she could move it away. A jolt of awareness tingled up her arm. She reminded herself to breathe and tugged her hand out from under his.

"Sorry." He offered an apologetic smile and turned back to the screen.

He scrolled past the first image—a blurry picture of his hand, taken when he reached to remove the SD card. The next two images appeared to be of nothing but scenery. Game cameras, intended to capture pictures of animals in the wild, could be tricky. When the sensor detected movement, the camera snapped a photo. The wind blowing a leaf or, in this case, a bullet zooming past could activate the camera.

Impatience swelled inside her. She reached forward to click to the next picture, but Sawyer once again grasped the mouse before she could. "Let's take it one at a time. I really want to… Wait a minute." He zoomed in on the image.

"What is it? What do you see?"

"There in the corner." He pointed. A side view of the shooter, barely in the frame. His head turned away from the camera, and a rifle in his left hand.

Sawyer clicked to print the image, and then he picked up a pen and reached for the notepad on the corner of the desk. Across the top of the page, he wrote *Facts About the Shooter*. Beneath that he wrote *dark hair, slender build.*

As he worked, Bridget thought about the man beside her. He had done all the right things to keep them safe earlier. And he had been so precise in the things he did, including the way he shot a gun. Several times over the last few weeks, his mannerisms had seemed reminiscent of someone in law enforcement and not a typical ranch foreman. He didn't even walk with the normal swagger of a cowboy. Instead, he walked with squared shoulders and long, confident strides.

Just how well did her grandparents know this man they'd left in charge of their ranch?

Sawyer scrolled through the next couple of photos, stopping when he came to an image taken the day before that appeared to be a random picture of nothing followed by an image of a doe. "Well, that's it. Looks like we didn't get a picture of this guy's face." He pushed away from the computer. "I'll finish scrolling through these images later. Right now, let's try to figure out what this guy was up to and why he was shooting at us."

"Isn't that the section of property where Granddad wants to build a small two-bedroom cabin?"

"That's right. We put the game cameras out last spring. Your grandfather is thinking about renting the cabin out to hunters during deer and turkey seasons, and hopefully, in the off-seasons, he can rent to families who want to unplug from their busy lifestyles. We've been checking the cameras weekly to see if there's enough game to support such a venture."

Bridget pulled the mouse closer and started clicking keys. "Do you think this guy could be a poacher?"

"That's possible." He rubbed his jaw and tapped the pen on the pad of paper. "Okay, so our guy is of average height. He was about a head taller than the post, so he's around five foot ten. We also know he's—"

"Wow! Beautiful. Two bucks and a doe in one shot." She gasped at the splendor of the picture taken yesterday in the same location where someone had tried to kill them less than two hours ago. The picture reminded her of her therapist's instructions to find something positive in every situation. Bridget had even made a sign that she'd taped to her bedroom mirror that read, *In the darkest moments, look for the light and embrace everyday beauty.*

Sawyer leaned toward the monitor, his shoulder brushing hers, and pointed at the picture with the tip of his pen. "That ten-point buck has been coming around every couple of days since we first put out the cameras, but the others have only recently joined him."

She clicked the back arrow a few times. The smaller buck and the doe moved positions in each photo, but the ten-point buck stayed in the background, scraping at the dirt with his antlers. "That's strange. What's he found?"

"I'm not sure. Zoom in."

She did as instructed. "It looks like a… grave."

Bridget rapidly clicked through the photos, going backward in time, desperate to uncover the source of the dirt mound. Her chest tightened with each click, threatening to suffocate her.

"Slow down." Sawyer placed his hand over hers, stilling her movements for a moment. "We don't want to miss any clues in our haste."

"We can scroll back through after we get to the start."

"I know. And we will. But I'd like to see the images without any preconceived ideas."

She looked at him, sure that her face must convey her confusion. "Who are you? What did you do before you came to work for my grandparents?"

He closed his eyes. Was he praying, or was he trying to come up with a cover story? A few moments later, he sighed and opened his eyes. "Your grandfather knows my past. If at some point it becomes imperative for you to know, I'll tell you. Until then, can we just focus on finding the person who shot at us?"

She opened her mouth to argue, thought better of it and pressed her lips tight. He was right. It was none of her business. Granddad wouldn't have hired Sawyer if he didn't trust him. Turning back to the laptop, she clicked to see the next picture. "That's—"

"The guy who shot at us," they said in unison.

The man in the photo was walking away from the camera, but his baseball cap, hair color and build were the same.

"He has a shovel in his right hand." Sawyer pointed to the screen.

"But he held his rifle with his left hand. Wouldn't he carry the shovel with his dominant hand?"

"He could be ambidextrous." Sawyer scribbled on his notepad. "Only ten percent of the population is left-handed. Less than one percent of the population is ambidextrous. But I doubt this clue is going to help us much."

The next few photos showed their shooter digging the hole, dragging a black bag from a spot outside the camera's view, putting it into the hole and covering it with dirt. The entire time, the unknown man kept his back to the camera. Like he knew it was there.

The date and time stamp showed the photos were taken three days earlier, in the late afternoon. The total time between the man's arrival and departure was four hours and twenty-three minutes. He hadn't been in a hurry. It was as if he knew no one would come along and catch him.

"We need to call the sheriff." Bridget's voice sounded shrill, even to her own ears. "He's going to be angry that we didn't call him sooner. It's already dark out. It'll be after nine o'clock by the time he gets here."

"What was there to report until now?" Sawyer pulled his cell phone out of his pocket. "Besides, he wouldn't have been able to look at the pictures any quicker than we did."

Seriously? Why was he being so calm? Bridget jumped out of her seat, causing the desk chair to roll backward into the wall. "I'm pretty sure the guy wasn't burying treasure. There's a good chance a body is in that bag. What if the shooter's already gone back and moved it? We should have driven into town and turned the SD card over to Sheriff Rice instead of looking at it ourselves first."

Bridget hadn't realized she was pacing until firm hands grasped her by the shoulders and pulled her around to come face-to-face with hazel eyes, the same color as her ex-boyfriend's. Only these eyes were mesmerizing.

Men with hazel eyes had always made her heart beat a little faster. *You don't think we can continue with our relationship now, do you?* The last words her ex had said on his way out of her hospital room echoed in her memory. *Don't you know every man wants a biological child? A son that looks like him, who can carry on the family name. You can't give me that now.*

"Stop pacing. And breathe."

Pulled from her wayward thoughts, she tried to focus on what he was saying. "Huh?"

"I said stop pacing and breathe." He pushed a hand through his wavy brown hair. "You talk faster than anyone I've ever met. Do you ever stop for air?"

"Sorry. I naturally talk fast, but it's worse when I'm nervous. Or worried. Like now." She sank into the chair. "I'm a rule follower. I do things by the book. Why did I let you talk me into looking at the pictures before calling the sheriff? We've wasted so much time…"

"Exactly. It was my idea. Not yours. I'll take full responsibility."

"Unfortunately, life doesn't work that way. We have to take responsibility for our own actions. I'll face the repercussions head-on, and I won't hide behind you." She nodded at the phone still clutched in his hand. "Go ahead, call Sheriff Rice so we can get back out there and dig up that bag."

Sawyer glanced at his watch as the team of sheriff department ATVs appeared over the ridge, kicking up a trail of dust as they approached. Since there had been some concern that the shooter might return and dig up the grave, the sheriff had agreed that Sawyer should return to the site and stand guard until they arrived.

He had tried to return alone, but Bridget wouldn't hear of it, insisting they employ her grandfather's rule to use the buddy system, especially this late at night. Since her family owned the ranch and he was merely an employee, he'd felt like he had no choice but to agree. Besides, it was never a bad idea to have backup in a situation like this.

"Sheriff Rice, please tell me your men have a lead on the guy who shot at us," Sawyer demanded as soon as the quartet of law enforcement officials pulled to a stop.

"Not yet. But we will. I forwarded the photos you faxed me to every sheriff in a one-hundred-mile radius. Also, the description you gave me of the ATV he was driving matches one reported stolen from Stone Bridge Farm. We found it in a ditch about two miles up the road. Hopefully, we'll be able to lift some prints off of it."

The sheriff turned his attention to the deputies he'd brought with him, motioning for them to park in a semicircle around the perimeter of the crime scene. Spotlights attached to the hoods of their ATVs bathed the area in a bright light.

"Now, you two, stay out of the way while we examine the area and determine if there's any need for alarm."

Sawyer refrained from saying what he thought of the sheriff's words. He wondered if the sheriff's attitude toward him would be a little less condescending if he knew about his law enforcement training and background.

No. It was best to step back and let the local authorities handle the situation. This wasn't his jurisdiction. Besides, Sawyer refused to get dragged back into that life one minute sooner than he was ready, if ever.

He shrugged out of his denim jacket and spread it on the ground under a nearby tree, and grasped Bridget's elbow to help her sit. She shook her head and tried to move away. "No arguments. Your grandparents would probably fire me if I let you catch a cold."

She smiled. "You're probably right. Thank you."

"You're welcome." He sat on the ground beside her, ignoring the slight chill that seeped through his jeans from the cold ground.

The deputies canvassed the area on both sides of the fence with handheld torchlights, taking photos of tire tracks and footprints, as well as the dirt mound and the front fender of the Gator, while Sheriff Rice examined the grave.

Bridget absentmindedly picked at her nail polish. "I wish they'd hurry."

Sawyer covered the hand that rested on top of her knee, stopping her fidgeting. Something he wouldn't normally do. But this wasn't an ordinary day. "They have to get pictures before they disturb anything. Be patient, a little longer."

"It's hard to be patient not knowing what we'll find."

A cool mountain breeze blew through the trees, and she shivered. He rubbed her hand, trying to offer what warmth he could. "You know, I could probably get a deputy to drive you back to the house and stay with you. Then, you could—"

"No. I'm fine."

He knew better, regardless of what she said. She hadn't been fine all evening. Not from the moment they first entered the woods, long before their attacker fired the first shot.

"Sheriff, we're all clear," an officer yelled from across the field.

She pulled her hand from Sawyer's when the sheriff walked over to them. "Okay, let's see what our guy buried." He eyed Bridget. "Why don't you wait here."

She bristled. "If you don't mind, I'd rather not. I promise to stay out of everyone's way."

"Suit yourself." Sheriff Rice turned and crossed to the mound of dirt, leaving them to follow him. "Zack, I want you to walk the fence line. We don't want this guy to sneak up on us in the dark. Caleb and Pete will take turns digging."

"I can dig, too, Sheriff," Sawyer volunteered, wanting to speed up the process.

Sheriff Rice nodded. "Fine. We want to get this done as quickly as possible, but we also want to preserve any evidence. So, I want you to dig a trench on the right side of the mound and then pull the dirt from the mound into the trench. Got it?"

"Yes, sir," the men said in unison.

"Good. Now, Ms. Vincent, why don't you and I stand over here out of the way."

Forty-five minutes later, Sawyer wiped his brow with the back of his arm. Sweat poured down his back despite the cool temps. He pulled his cell phone out of his pocket and checked the time. Ten forty-three. He nodded to Caleb to take over, climbed out of the trench and headed to the cooler for a bottle of water.

Bridget walked over to him, an oversize jacket draped across her shoulders. "Nice jacket."

"Apparently, I looked cold. Sheriff Rice told me I had to wear his jacket, or he'd force me to go home and wait."

Sawyer heard the frustration in her voice. "Don't enjoy taking orders, do you?"

"With five brothers, I've done it all my life. So, no, not really."

"I'm sure the sheriff meant well."

"I know—"

"Sheriff, we've found the black bag."

Dropping the plastic water bottle, Sawyer grasped Bridget's hand and pulled her along with him back to the edge of the large pit that had been dug. Pete held a spotlight, illuminating a black garment bag, while Caleb snapped pictures.

The officers each donned a pair of gloves. Then the sheriff motioned for Caleb to unzip the bag. Almost immediately, the strong stench of death wafted into the air.

Sawyer was vaguely aware of Bridget turning away from the scene, falling to her knees and heaving. But he couldn't do anything to help her. His eyes were transfixed by the sight before him. A sight he'd seen nine previous times.

Female. Caucasian. Midtwenties. Strawberry blond hair. Wearing a white lacy dress. A crown of pink and white silk roses on her head. But something was different this time.

He sucked in a deep breath, the cool air burning his lungs. Tucked under her stiff, decomposing hands was a manila envelope. Addressed to Special Agent Sawyer Eldridge.

Ready or not, it looked like Sawyer was going back to his life as a profiler. Lovelorn, the serial killer who made him second-guess his ability as a profiler and whom he thought had died eighteen months ago, was alive. And had claimed another victim.

TWO

Bridget covered her mouth and nose, desperate to block the suffocating stench. She crawled several feet away, grasped a tree and pulled herself upright. The Gator UTV that she and Sawyer had driven sat to her right. Experience had taught her the foreman was always prepared, so she ran to the UTV and dug in the small glove compartment, one hand still clutched over her face. Seconds later, she pulled a red handkerchief out of the small opening. She found a bottle of water in the cooler. Holding her breath, she removed the hand that had been blocking the smell and poured the cool liquid over the square of cloth, wrung it out and quickly pressed it to her mouth and nose. She didn't know if this would work to block the stench, but she'd seen it done many times in the movies to block smoke from entering the lungs. If nothing else, the cool, damp cloth felt good against her clammy skin, and that alone might be enough to hold back the gag reflex long enough for her to go look at the body.

Bridget wasn't normally squeamish. However, since that day eight months ago when Robert Covington, the estranged husband of one of her clients, stabbed her multiple times and left her for dead, strong odors made her queasy. She blamed it on the overpowering smells she'd had to endure during her extended hospital stay. Rubbing alcohol. Disinfectant. Hand sanitizers.

She shuddered and turned back to the open grave.

The sheriff paced the area around the pit as he barked orders into his radio. "Get the coroner out here, ASAP. And call Thomas. Tell him we need the K9 unit."

Hunched together, Caleb and Pete photographed the body. Mesmerized, Bridget inched closer, following the movement of the camera. White lettering on the bag identified it as being from a high-end boutique on the affluent side of Knoxville. A wreath of pink and white silk roses on the victim's head looked strangely alive and vibrant in contrast to the scene. Delicate lace at the neckline of the white dress. Perhaps a wedding dress? Lifeless hands folded over a manila envelope with bold black print. *Special Agent Sawyer Eldridge.*

Bridget's head jerked upward, and she searched the perimeter as she fought to push air into her lungs. Where was *Special Agent* Sawyer Eldridge? She spotted him standing in the shadows at the edge of the pool of light circling the crime scene, his face hidden in darkness. He turned in her direction, and though she couldn't see them, she felt his eyes on her for the briefest moment before he looked away.

Anger bubbled up inside her. She'd specifically asked him about his past, but he'd refused to share information with her. And now some maniac was burying bodies and leaving notes for *Special Agent* Sawyer Eldridge. How could he bring this kind of trouble to her grandparents' home?

Bridget followed Sawyer's every movement as she made her way over to where he stood. He held his cell phone to his ear with his right hand while he alternated between shoving his left hand through his hair and clutching it into a fist at his side. He spoke in hushed, urgent tones, unaware of her approach. "Fly down here. If it's not him, go back home and leave the investigation to the local authorities. But if it is *him*, you'll be glad you got here sooner, rather than later... Yes... I'll text you the photos I snapped."

A twig broke under her foot. Sawyer looked over his shoulder, and his gaze locked on hers as he spoke into the phone. "Just get here. Fast."

He disconnected the call, pushed a few buttons on his phone and stepped into the light. He looked as tired as she felt. Haggard eyes and hunched shoulders seemed to emphasize the weight of the situation unfolding around them. His grim expression tugged at her heart, and her anger evaporated. She took a step toward him, then halted. A soft gasp escaped her lips. Had she really been about to hug this man? To offer him comfort? Her mind reeled. He'd kept his identity a secret, and a murderer sent him a message on a dead body. No telling what else he was hiding. Could he be trusted?

Sawyer closed the distance between them and pulled the handkerchief away from her face. His smile softened his eyes. "Creative thinking. Did it help?"

She nodded, her throat too dry for words to form.

"I guess it's imperative now, huh?" His voice sounded husky. "Time for you to know who I am. My past."

"I'd like to know that myself." They jumped and turned to face the sheriff, standing a few feet away. A notepad, held in his right hand, tapped an unknown beat on his left palm. "Bridget, if you'll excuse us, I have a few questions for Mr. Eldridge."

Bridget found her voice. "I think I'll stick around, if you don't mind."

She looked to Sawyer for agreement. His phone dinged. He pulled it out and read the message on the screen, then put it away again.

Smiling, he placed the handkerchief back into her hand and lifted it to her face. Then he grasped her elbow and guided her past the sheriff. "I'll answer all the questions either of you have once the crime scene has been processed."

"Now look here, I don't think you're in any position to—"

Sawyer paused, pulled his wallet out of his back pocket, flipped it open and showed it to Sheriff Rice. "My credentials. You'll receive a phone call shortly from Deputy Director Taylor Williams telling you when to expect his arrival. This has officially become an FBI investigation. We would appreciate your full cooperation."

He turned back to her, his features softening. "I know you have a million questions, and I'll answer all the ones I can. But for now, I'd appreciate it if you'd go sit under the tree or wait in the Gator until I'm finished here."

His words left no room for argument. For the first time since she met him, Bridget saw the real Sawyer Eldridge. Like the cartoon superheroes she'd watched as a child, the man before her had transformed from an ordinary, hardworking ranch hand into a no-nonsense, take-charge federal agent right before her eyes.

Hours later, as the early rays of sunshine crept over the Appalachian Mountains, Sawyer pulled his phone out of his pocket. Six fifty-seven. He scanned the crowd and found Bridget sitting against the large oak tree. Her head rested on her arms, and he wondered if she was asleep. If so, it was a sign of how truly exhausted she was.

In addition to the original law enforcement officers who'd descended on the area, there were now two agents from the Knoxville FBI field office at the scene, along with the medical examiner and his assistant.

The sheriff and Special Agent in Charge Davis Anderson stood to one side of the group, talking in muffled tones, their notebooks open as they compared notes. Sawyer had to give Sheriff Rice credit. The sheriff had instructed his men to cooperate any way they could, then he'd glued himself to the side of Agent Anderson. He'd stepped back and let the FBI take over the investigation without a lot of fuss.

Sawyer crossed to where the men stood. "Gentlemen. Bridget and I need to head back to the farmhouse. Deputy Director Williams will arrive in a little over an hour."

"The medical examiner is getting ready to remove the body. We've bagged all the evidence—including the note to you, which I'll bring to the house when I leave here. There wasn't any identifying information with the body. No driver's license. College ID. Nothing. We'll run her prints, but there's no guarantee we'll get a hit." Agent Anderson nodded toward the sheriff. "Sheriff Rice doesn't think the victim is from Barton Creek. There have been no missing person reports. According to the time stamp on the photos and the condition of the body, we know she's been missing three days, if not longer."

"Her name is Isabella Harris." The three men turned at the sound of Bridget's voice. She gave a half shrug, a frown on her face. "I've been sitting over there trying to figure out why she looked so familiar. The last time

I saw her was over nine years ago when she dropped out of school and moved to Nashville with dreams of becoming a country music star. Grams heard she moved back to the area. She worked at a diner over in Maryville. I stopped in there a couple of weeks ago for lunch to see her, but I was told she worked nights."

She turned and looked at Sawyer questioningly. "Remember, I told you about running into the investment banker who wanted to know if I thought Granddad would ever be interested in selling the ranch. He kept going on and on and got me so flustered I forgot to leave my cell phone number for Isabella. I had planned to go back another time, but..."

The sadness in her voice tied Sawyer's gut into knots, and apprehension washed over him. "How can you be sure it's Isabella?"

"The medical examiner shifted the body while he was taking photos—I guess so he could check for injuries or bruising, I don't know. Anyway, when he turned her head, I saw a birthmark on the back of her neck. It's a port-wine birthmark. In the shape of Italy."

He reached for Bridget's hand and asked softly, "How do you know her?"

Tormented emerald eyes met his. "Her parents used to own a farm a few miles up the road. When we'd come visit our grandparents for the summer, we'd always hang out with her. She even dated my brother. She was practically family."

Sawyer knew Bridget was an only daughter with five brothers. Charlie, Nate and Ryan were older than her, and Hoyt and Ethan were younger. "Which brother?"

"Hoyt. He and Ethan are twins. Ethan is a missionary in Tanzania, and Hoyt is an—"

"FBI agent," they said in unison.

Her eyes widened. "You know Hoyt?"

"We need to get to the house. I'll explain things on the way." Only just realizing he still held her hand, Sawyer reluctantly let go and turned back to the officers, whom he'd almost forgotten. "We'll be expecting you back at the house. I'll have the coffee waiting."

As he guided Bridget back to the UTV, the morning sun chased away the remnants of darkness. A family of raccoons ran in and out of a fallen log on the other side of the fence line. Sawyer wondered at the stark contrast of the playful animals with the scene of death in the background.

"Do you always do that?" Bridget's voice interrupted his thoughts.

"Do what?"

"Take over. Like telling the sheriff and

Agent Anderson to meet you at the house and you'll have coffee ready. Kind of like you're in charge."

"I wasn't trying to step on your toes, boss lady."

She turned, a frown on her face, as he held the UTV door for her. "I wasn't asking because it upset me. I simply wondered if it was a personality trait."

"You like to figure people out, don't you?"

Bridget shrugged, one hand on her hip, the other on the roof of the vehicle. "I'm learning there's usually more to people than what you see on the surface."

How many times in the past had people let her down because she didn't truly know them? There was much to learn about this beautiful woman, but it would have to wait.

"I was raised an only child by a single, working mother, so I had to learn to take charge at an early age. I won't apologize for it." He smiled. "But I promise to try not to be so heavy-handed about it. Okay?"

Sawyer held out his hand to indicate that she should get into the vehicle.

After she was seated, he jogged around to the other side, climbed in beside her and started the engine.

"How did you—"

"Did Hoyt—" They spoke in unison.

If he wanted her to answer his questions, he needed to give her the same courtesy. "Ladies first."

Bridget twisted in her seat, pulling one leg up and tucking it under the other. "What is your position with the FBI? How did you meet Hoyt? Did he get you the job at the ranch? Are you working undercover? Do my grandparents know you're an FBI agent?"

"Behavior Analysis Unit. At the academy. Yes. No. And, of course."

She puffed out a breath of air. "Could you elaborate? Please."

"For two years, I worked on a case profiling a serial killer named Lovelorn. Each year, Lovelorn increased his number of victims by one. It was the fourth year of his killing spree, and nine women were dead. Six in the first three years. Three that year. Which meant that another woman would die before the end of the year. There was a guy—a law student—who fit the killer's profile."

"What happened?"

"As I was arriving home from work late one evening, I saw someone trying to abduct my neighbor outside her condo. My arrival scared the would-be abductor, and he got away. But he left behind a poem."

"A poem?"

"Lovelorn's calling card. Each one of his victims received a poem in the mail the day he killed them. Mary Kate is the only person to receive a poem from Lovelorn and escape." He glanced at Bridget. "Time to face forward and make sure your seat belt is snug."

Once she'd followed his directive, he shifted into four-wheel drive and guided the vehicle along the rutted path up the side of the mountain. "I arranged for Mary Kate to hide out at a safe house in Utah until we could catch Lovelorn. Agent Vicki Miller, who favored Mary Kate and the other victims, moved into Mary Kate's condo and went undercover as a law student. She kept the suspect under surveillance for three weeks.

"Then one foggy morning there was a pileup on the interstate. We found Agent Miller's body in the trunk of one car. The driver of the vehicle was dead. He was a professor at the law school. I'd overlooked him when I compiled a list of suspects. Our serial killer was dead. Case closed. After that, I started doubting my…contribution…to the Bureau." He hoped his raspy voice didn't betray how gut-wrenching this conversation was for him. "I transferred to a position at the academy where I taught a class on pathological behaviors."

"Hoyt mentioned that class. It was one of his favorites."

"Hoyt's class was the first and only group I taught. I needed a change. I had spent three summers working at a ranch in Colorado to help pay my way through college. When Hoyt mentioned your grandfather was looking for a new foreman, I applied for the job and took a year's leave of absence from my position at the Bureau."

"A one-year leave? That means your time at the ranch will be over in a couple of months?"

He wasn't ready to discuss his impending decision yet. Time to redirect her to the pressing matter at hand. "My turn to ask a question."

She raised an eyebrow. "Yes?"

"Did Hoyt keep in touch with Isabella?"

"No. To my knowledge, they haven't seen each other or spoken since the night they broke up."

"What happened that night? Do you know?"

She shook her head. "Hoyt's a very private person. He never wanted to talk about it."

"Nothing? You haven't heard anything in all these years?"

"Hoyt had a crush on Isabella from the moment he first laid eyes on her the summer before eighth grade. Two years later, they started dating, even maintaining a long-distance relationship through their junior year of high school. I really thought they would be together forever, but the next summer, they broke up."

Their conversation ended as the farmhouse came into view. Sawyer parked the UTV in the utility shed behind the barn. He turned off the engine, pocketed the key and shifted in his seat. "I've often wondered what it would have been like to have grown up with siblings. I wonder if Kayla would have respected my privacy the way you respected Hoyt's."

"Kayla?"

"My kid sister. Well, not so much a kid. She just celebrated her twenty-second birthday last month."

"If you have a sister, why don't you know what it's like to grow up with a sibling?" She furrowed her brow. "I thought you were an only child?"

How to explain his mixed-up family? There wasn't enough time left in the universe. "It's a long story. Suffice it to say, not all families are like yours. Some are broken. But that's a story for another time. Right now, we need to get inside and prepare for the arrival of my superior. And Hoyt."

"Hoyt's coming?"

"Deputy Director Williams thought it would be a good idea for him to come, since he's familiar with the area. This was to be his first major field assignment. Of course, Williams made that decision before we knew the identity of the victim. Unfortunately, with this recent development, Hoyt may be too close to the case to be allowed to stay on it."

Sawyer could only imagine how difficult it would be to work a case like this if he had once loved the victim. It had been bad enough having a coworker and friend murdered by Lovelorn, but while he had always respected Agent Miller, he hadn't been in love with her. Love would most definitely cloud an agent's judgment.

Bridget left Sawyer to make coffee and headed upstairs to call Ryan—her older brother and boss. Ryan and his friend Lincoln Jameson were co-owners of Protective Instincts, the security firm where she had been working as a bodyguard for the past four years.

None of her experience had prepared her for this. She needed Ryan here. Fast.

She pressed Call as soon as she crossed the threshold of her bedroom and sank to the floor to sit with her back against the bed the way she used to when she was younger.

Ryan answered on the third ring. "Wow, Peanut, you're up early. Are you getting up with the roosters, now? I imagine you're ready for Granddad and Grams to re—"

"Ryan. Something's happened. I need you here." Bridget's voice cracked, and she didn't even try to hide the emotion she was feeling. "Sawyer and I went to check the game cameras and a guy shot at us. Then we viewed the pictures on the SD card and discovered a grave. The stench was awful."

"Bridge."

"There was a letter to Sawyer. Did you know he's an FBI agent? And the body was Isabella Harris. Now Hoyt's on his way, but he won't be allowed to work the case because he dated the victim. How am I supposed to help him deal with the emotions he's going to experience over Isabella's murder? He'll be here any minute with the Deputy Direc—"

"Bridget!"

She stopped and gulped a breath of air.

"Slow down," her brother's authoritative voice commanded. "You're talking too fast.

I can't wrap my brain around everything that quickly."

People were always telling her to slow down or repeat things. She'd always talked too fast. As a child, her nickname was Motormouth. Her parents, teachers and siblings always accused her of speeding through life. She walked fast and talked faster, especially when she was tired, excited or stressed. At this moment, she was all three.

She sighed. "I'm sorry. I haven't had any sleep, and now…"

"It's okay, Bridge. Let me see what I understand. There was a trespasser. He shot at you and Sawyer. Then you found a grave with a body and a letter for Sawyer. And did I hear correctly, you think the body is Isabella Harris?"

"No. I know it's Isabella. I saw her birthmark." The tears that had burned and threatened all night spilled down her face. She scrubbed at them with the back of her hand, unable to halt the flow. "I'm sorry…just… When can you get here?"

"Bridge. I'm in Cancun. I got a lead on Troy, and I had to follow up on it."

"Cancun?" Ryan being out of the country didn't surprise her. He'd spent years and countless amounts of money trying to track down Troy Odom, the man who killed his fiancée, Jessica Jameson. A hiccup escaped, and she laughed to cover it up. "I guess it'll take longer than the normal four-hour flight to get here, huh?"

"Sorry, Bridge. I'll be there as—"

The phone was snatched out of her hand. Startled, she watched as Sawyer knelt in front of her and put the phone to his ear. "Ryan. It's Sawyer. Yes. I should have called you earlier… Yes… You can call him… I will… See you soon. Goodbye."

He disconnected the call and handed the phone back to her. "I got worried when you didn't come downstairs. I'm sorry about what I said earlier. The deputy director may allow Hoyt to stay on the case. Like you said, his relationship with Isabella was over long ago." He cupped her face in his right hand and swept his thumb under her eye. "I don't know what I was thinking. I should have known you were worried about your kid brother."

He tilted her chin upward. "Listen carefully. Whether Hoyt is allowed to stay on this case or not, he's going to be fine. And we will catch this guy."

"I know." She sniffled.

"The MO matches that of a known serial killer." He continued as if she hadn't spoken.

"One I thought was dead and buried, but I was wrong. I won't rest until I see him behind bars."

"It's Lovelorn, isn't it? He's alive, and he wants you to know it."

"Yes. I'm sorry. I promise I'll get him, this time."

The sound of vehicle tires crunching on the gravel drive penetrated the early morning quiet.

"Sounds like the cavalry has arrived." Sawyer stood and peered out the window before holding out his hand to Bridget and helping her up off the floor. "Hoyt and Deputy Director Williams are here. The sheriff and Agent Anderson pulled in behind them, but Sheriff Rice is getting into his car to leave."

"Agent Anderson's bringing the letter, right?"

"That's right." He nodded and headed for the door. Stopping in the doorway, he turned back to her. "You know, it's okay if you want to get some rest. You don't have to be a part of this. It doesn't have to affect you."

Oh, how she wished he were right. "You're wrong. It affects me. It affects my whole family." She walked past him and headed for the stairs. "This guy may be playing some sick game with you, but the minute he killed a family friend and buried her on the ranch, this became our fight, too. And, don't forget, he not only tried to kill you, he tried to kill me, too."

They reached the bottom of the stairs as Hoyt, Agent Anderson and a balding, middle-aged man with a paunchy stomach stepped through the front door.

"Hoyt!" Bridget raced down the last few steps and flung herself into her brother's arms. Hoyt gave her a quick squeeze, then pulled back.

"Hiya, Shorty," he said, his smile unable to conceal the sadness in his eyes.

Her heart ached to offer encouragement, but the words died on her lips. Her kid brother was a grown man. He didn't need her to soothe his heartaches. Especially with his boss standing two feet behind him.

"Gentlemen, we'll be working in the dining room. I've covered the table with trash bags so we can spread out the evidence without risk of contamination." Sawyer moved beside her and rested his hand on the small of her back, sending jolts of electricity through her as if she'd brushed against a live wire.

Hoyt stepped around them, obviously intent on doing as Sawyer had instructed, but came to a halt when the foreman put a detaining hand on his arm. Sawyer leaned in and spoke in hushed tones, then pulled back and, after a faint smile in her direction, led the other men out of the entryway.

Hoyt shook his head at the retreating backs before turning to her. "What's his deal? I mean, I know this is his case. I'm only a rookie, but—"

"Sawyer's a take-charge kind of guy. Something I guess we'll both have to get used to. What did he say to you?"

"He told me to take a few minutes and let my sister *mother* me, then we could join them." Hoyt grimaced. "You know I don't need mothering, right?"

Who knew Sawyer could be so thoughtful. He understood she was worried about her brother, and even though there was a murderer to catch, he was giving her a few minutes to ease her mind. Bridget smiled. "I know. But tell me, are you sure you want to work on this case? I mean, it's Isabella—"

Her six-foot-tall baby brother sat down on the second step of the stairs, caught her hand and pulled her down beside him. "Listen, Bridget. I understand. You mean well, but my relationship with Isabella ended nearly a decade ago. I know everyone thought Isabella was the love of my life. I almost bought into it myself, but we grew up. And apart. We had different dreams in life." He draped his arm across her shoulder. "I'm sad her life was cut short, and I'm angry at the way she died. But I won't crumble into a crying heap. I have a job to do. Helping to bring Isabella's killer to justice will be my way of honoring her."

Bridget noted the resolute expression on his face and the firm set of his jawline. Fine. She'd be a silent, supportive sister. Plastering a smile on her face, she wrapped her arm around his waist and gave him a hug. "Okay. I'll let it go. But remember, I'm here if you need to talk."

"Thanks for caring about me." He kissed the top of her head, then he stood and extended a hand to her.

"Let's go see what this guy's note says." She had taken two steps before the sound of a vehicle coming up the drive drew her attention. "Looks like the ranch hands are arriving. I'll go let them know Sawyer's going to be occupied today, so they'll have to take care of things on their own. Then I'll be in to see what this guy said in his note."

Hoyt halted her. "Let me check it out first." He unsnapped the holster at his waist and stepped onto the porch.

Bridget followed close behind. "See, it's just Joe and Smitty."

"So it is." He snapped the strap back over his gun. "Go deliver your message, but don't be out there long." Hoyt bent to her level. "After that, go upstairs and get some rest. I'll take care of things now that I'm here. No need for you to worry."

There it was. The automatic overprotective instinct that every Vincent brother seemed to possess. At one time, she'd thought it was a genetic flaw that they were born with. But even Ryan, the nonbiological brother, had similar tendencies. Although he'd eventually lightened up enough to hire her to work as a bodyguard.

She had found great satisfaction proving herself very capable as a bodyguard, despite her size. At least, until Robert's attack caught her off guard. But she would never let something like that happen again. Ever.

THREE

"The only reason I'm letting you look at the letter here instead of back at the office is because of the urgency of the situation. Honestly, we should—"

"I know." Sawyer hated to interrupt his superior, but patience had never been one of his virtues. He'd wasted enough time while filling the deputy director in on the events of the past fifteen hours. He couldn't wait a moment longer to find answers. If the professor who had died in the car crash wasn't Lovelorn, who was? What was the professor's connection to the serial killer? And where had the killer been for the last eighteen months? "If the killer *is* Lovelorn, we'll need every second we can get to catch him."

A thought hit Sawyer. "What about Mary Kate Newman? Since she was Lovelorn's last known target, we probably need to let her know he's still alive."

"You may remember, even though we thought she was no longer in danger, Mary Kate decided to stay in Salt Lake City instead of returning to her life in Chicago. I felt a responsibility to her, so I asked our office in Billings to keep a check on her." The deputy director offered a half smile. "Right now, Mary Kate is safe and sound and currently in Hawaii on her honeymoon. She and her husband—one of the field agents in Salt Lake—aren't expected to return home for another week."

"Well, that's good news at least." Sawyer sighed. "Let's hope we can catch this creep before their honeymoon is over."

A creak sounded in the doorway, and relief surged through Sawyer when he saw Bridget lean against the doorframe, concerned eyes following her brother's movements as he viewed the shell casings recovered at the scene.

He'd been worried when Hoyt had entered the room without her earlier. Sawyer caught Bridget's eye and cocked an eyebrow at her. She smiled and gave a slight nod. They'd worked well together over the course of the last few weeks, often communicating with few words, as they'd learned to read each other's body language. Obviously, the talk went well, although Sawyer could tell by the way her eyes followed her brother's movements that she wasn't finished worrying.

He pulled on the pair of latex gloves Williams handed him. "Give me another pair, would you?"

"What for?"

"Ms. Vincent. Look. I know you'd prefer I send her out of the room," Sawyer rushed on when his boss opened his mouth to object, interrupting his superior twice in one morning. "But she's been involved from the moment the first shot rang out. I will not leave her out of this."

"Are you determined to break every rule in the book on this case?" The veteran agent shook his head. "You haven't changed one bit, have you? You still think as long as you reach the right outcome the means of getting there doesn't matter."

Sawyer remained silent. No point answering the obvious.

"Fine. Let's stop wasting time." Williams handed him the extra pair of gloves.

Sawyer crossed the room to Bridget. "Where have you been?"

"In the barn. I had to get the guys started on their chores for the day."

"What was Hoyt thinking letting you

go out there by yourself? Listen to me. I don't want you wandering around on your own until we capture this guy." He knew he sounded harsh, but he was worried. Why in the world would she act as if nothing had happened when there was a serial killer on the loose? "Put these on. But don't touch anything without permission."

"Yes, sir." Playful sarcasm laced her words.

"I'm not trying to be bossy, just efficient. Agent Williams would rather open the letter without you present, but I figure you earned the right to be here the instant this killer took a shot at you. So." He gave a pointed look at the gloves. "Can you do as I ask?"

"Yes. I'll put on the gloves and not touch anything without permission." She snapped the gloves into place and followed him across the room, where they joined the others already gathered around the evidence.

The letter lay in the center of the table, like a beacon warning of danger. Sawyer picked up the plastic evidence bag and extracted the manila envelope. Then he took the pocket-knife Hoyt offered and slit open the flap. His gaze swept around the group before coming to rest on Bridget.

Her porcelain skin seemed paler than usual. She had to be exhausted after staying up all night at the dig site. Perhaps he had been wrong to insist she be present for this reveal.

She frowned and nodded at the envelope clasped in his hand, obviously anxious to see what it contained.

Too late now. He puffed out a breath and pushed the edges of the envelope in slightly so he could see inside. There appeared to be three sheets of paper. Holding the top edge of the page, he tugged the first sheet from the envelope and dropped it onto the table for everyone to see. Bold black print on a white sheet of paper jumped out at him.

Last time, you helped my target flee.
That won't happen again, believe me.
Sweet revenge is my ultimate goal.
When I'm done, you'll be a tortured soul.
This time I've brought an option or two.
Which will you take to eternity with you?

The proof he'd been seeking leaped off the page. The note rhymed. A signature MO of the Lovelorn killer. And a detail they'd purposefully left out of the press.

"He plans to kill you." Bridget's soft feminine voice broke the silence.

Sawyer shrugged. "I'm used to having a target on my back. It goes with the job."

"What about the person he plans to kill with you? Are they used to having a target on their back?" She bit her lip and then sighed. "I'm sorry. I shouldn't have said that."

"Your questions are reasonable. I'm sure they aren't used to being targeted by a killer. Which is why we need to stop him before he strikes again."

Agent Anderson cleared his throat and leaned across the table as he tried to peer inside the envelope still clutched in Sawyer's hand. "Is there anything else?"

Though Sawyer dreaded taking the other two sheets of paper out of the envelope, he knew he couldn't postpone the inevitable. Time to see the pictures of the women Lovelorn had targeted for this kill. In one full sweep, he withdrew the photos and dropped them onto the table. One was of a blond-haired, blue-eyed girl with a gentle soul who had taught him all about love and forgiveness and would always own a chunk of his heart. The other was of a petite, redheaded pixie with a spunky spirit who spoke her mind and stirred emotions in Sawyer that made him feel protective.

A gasp from the petite redhead rent the air.

Bridget's face stared back at her from the depths of a glossy eight-by-ten photo. She wore a green plaid shirt, her favorite brown palm-leaf cowboy hat and a schoolgirl grin. A faint blush added color to her makeup-free face. Even though the image was a headshot, she knew the exact moment the photo had been taken. Five days earlier. The day after her grandparents left on their vacation, when she'd helped corral the horses.

She'd brushed her glove-covered hand across her face, leaving a trail of mud behind, and Sawyer had taken out a handkerchief and wiped the dirt away. When she'd thanked him for being so gallant, he'd taken a sweeping bow and proclaimed to be at her service. The entire time they'd been goofing off, a serial killer had been close enough to take pictures.

Bridget's breath caught, and her throat constricted as if someone had tightened a noose around her neck. She was suffocating. "Th-that's…me."

Hoyt tugged her arm and pulled her around to face him. "Breathe." He placed his hands on each side of her face, forcing her to make eye contact. "Listen to me. It's going to be okay. We—I—won't let him near you. I'll keep you safe."

She pulled away from her brother, faintly aware of the murmuring going on around her.

She knew Hoyt couldn't keep his promise. He might want to be her protector, but he hadn't seen Isabella's body. Bridget had. If Lovelorn wanted her dead, it would take more than her brother's love and determination to stop him.

Tears of anger burned to be released, but she tamped them down, refusing to give way to her fear. No. Bridget was a survivor. Hadn't she proved so months earlier when she'd crawled to the highway that ran perpendicular to the running trail and attracted the attention of a passing motorist? She'd lost so much blood, the doctor had said she would have died if she'd been even five minutes later reaching the hospital. Three surgeries and countless hours of physical therapy later, and she had finally regained her strength. And now, another threat to her life. What had she done to deserve this? This could not be happening.

"Miss Vincent, we'll set you up in a safe house," Deputy Director Williams addressed her. But she didn't have time for his nonsense. Her mind was on one person, and one person alone. Sawyer.

Bridget turned to the man who'd brought this danger to their doorstep. The man she'd been building a friendship with the past couple of months. A friendship she'd thought had grown stronger as they'd worked the ranch together for the past week in her grandparents' absence. The man who'd hidden his true identity from her. Not a friend. A stranger. Someone she couldn't begin to understand. "Why would this killer target me? You're the one who brought him here."

Sawyer stood stoically, his eyes focused on the table. A muscle twitched in his jaw. She followed his gaze and, for the first time, noticed the second picture that had been in the envelope. A young woman, with shoulder-length, wavy blond hair, smiled at something off camera. Her eyes shone, her face exuding happiness.

Dear God, how could I have been so self-absorbed? The killer brought "an option or two." If he doesn't kill me, he's going to kill her.

What was this woman's connection to Sawyer or the case? "Who is she?"

Her question seemed to snap him out of his trance. "My half sister, Kayla." He pulled out his cell phone, punching numbers as he continued. "She's a student at NYU. Come on, Kayla, answer."

With a groan, he jerked the phone away from his ear and started typing a text message.

Agent Anderson punched numbers into his

cell phone and commanded, "Give me her address. I'll send an officer to check on her and move her to a safe place."

Sawyer rattled off the address, then started scrolling through his contacts as Anderson walked out of the room. "I'll try her roommate."

Bridget picked up the photo. There was a concrete tower in the background. "Clingmans Dome."

"What was that?" Sawyer pulled the photo out of her grasp. "Hey, I thought I told you not to touch anything."

"Sawyer, look at the background. The concrete walkway and tower are located inside the Great Smoky Mountains National Park. When was the last time Kayla visited you? Could this have been taken then?"

"Kayla's never been here. She's planning a trip in the spring after she graduates. We're going to hike a portion of the Appalachian Trail."

"We have officers en route to your sister's apartment. We'll get her to safety."

Without breaking eye contact with Bridget, Sawyer replied to his supervisor, "They won't find her there. He already has her. Tell them to treat her apartment like a crime scene."

Hoyt had stood quietly beside Bridget looking over each piece of evidence. He picked up the envelope and looked inside. "There's another piece of paper in here."

Turning the envelope upside down, he shook it until a half sheet of paper floated to the table displaying another message from the killer.

Ticktock, time is flying like a bird.
You have until midnight on the twenty-third,
That is unless you've lost your touch.
Will this challenge be too much?
Or can you save one of these damsels in distress.
From being my next model in a wedding dress?

The twenty-third. Wednesday. The day Bridget's entire family would arrive at the ranch for the Thanksgiving holiday weekend.

With all of her siblings scattered about different places, building careers and some with families of their own, it had been a few years since everyone had been together. This year, they had all agreed to rearrange their schedules to be at their grandparents' ranch to celebrate and give extra thanks that Bridget was still with them. A shiver raced along her spine. If Lovelorn gets his way, she'll be dead before Thanksgiving.

"Today's the twentieth." Sawyer's heart constricted as if someone had put it in a vise grip. "We only have two and a half days to find Kayla."

"Sir, wouldn't midnight Wednesday be three and a half days?" Hoyt questioned.

Sawyer shook his head. "No. In military time, midnight is zero hundred. The beginning of the day. So, *midnight on the twenty-third* would be in the middle of the night Tuesday evening, not Wednesday." He picked up the photo of Kayla. "I'm sure Lovelorn knows this. But he hopes we overlook that detail. Because then we'd be twenty-four hours too late to save my sister."

Why hadn't he checked the game camera sooner? If he hadn't got behind schedule, he would have had more time to find her.

Please, Lord, let me get to Kayla before it's too late. We spent too many years separated. I need more time with her.

"We'll find her." A small hand slid into his, and a jolt of awareness coursed through his body. Bridget. She couldn't be here. He had to get her to safety.

"Agent Vincent, I need you to transport your sister to a safe house. Deputy Dir—"

"I'm not going to a safe house. I'm staying here and helping find your sister."

Frustration boiled inside him. "No. You're. Not."

The little spitfire stretched to her full height and squared her shoulders. "You seem to forget. I'm his other target. So, I have a say in this."

He had to make her understand the danger she was in. "That's exactly why you don't have a say. Your life depends on following my instructions. Besides, how can I save Kayla if I'm worried about keeping you safe, too?"

"How can you save her without me? Lovelorn is obviously watching us. I know Granddad. He has a schedule for every chore on this ranch. You said it yourself. You got behind checking those cameras. I guarantee Lovelorn knew which day you normally went to the back forty. It's not a coincidence he buried Isabella the day before you were supposed to check the cameras. So, my question to you is, if I suddenly disappear, what's keeping him from killing Kayla sooner than planned?"

"That won't happen." How could he make her understand he needed to know she was safe? He didn't want to lose either woman.

Not the sister he was still getting to know, nor Bridget, the beautiful woman with the infectious laugh and mischievous smile who made him long for things he knew he could never have.

He'd never had many close friends. The few colleagues he had thought were friends erased themselves from his life when he faced the inquisition following Agent Miller's murder. Sawyer hadn't blamed his colleagues for distancing themselves from him. After all, if he hadn't profiled the wrong person as the killer, Agent Miller would still be alive. His insistence that the law student was Lovelorn had kept everyone focused on the wrong person, allowing the real Lovelorn to kill Miller.

Sawyer still couldn't believe he hadn't been found guilty of any wrongdoing. Even so, he'd decided it was best to be a loner so he couldn't let others down. He'd shut himself off the past year, not getting close to anyone, treating his bosses and the other ranch hands as mere acquaintances. Then, two months ago, this pixie waltzed into his world and made him start enjoying the little things in life again. He'd laughed at her jokes while finding excuses to prolong the time they spent together doing chores.

"I hate to admit it, Sawyer, but Miss Vincent is right." Deputy Director Williams rubbed his chin.

"Sir, you want to put my sister in jeopardy?" Hoyt questioned. "I don't think—"

"That's enough, Agent. Of course I don't want to put your sister in jeopardy. We'll have agents—including you—looking out for her." Beads of sweat glistened on the older man's bald head, and he blotted the surface with a handkerchief. "Now I need you to go see what Agent Anderson found out about Agent Eldridge's sister."

Lines appeared around Hoyt's mouth, and his shoulders slumped slightly as he turned to obey. Sawyer felt bad for the rookie, knowing Hoyt never would have spoken to a superior in such a manner if he hadn't been concerned about his sister's safety.

As soon as Hoyt was out of earshot, Sawyer faced his superior and Bridget. "This guy's history clearly proves he doesn't like his routine disturbed. Even if something changes—like Bridget being taken outside his reach—he isn't likely to change his plans."

"Isn't likely? Doesn't mean he won't." Bridget met his gaze, her eyes full of compassion. "Are you willing to take that chance with your sister's life?"

"Fine." He caved. "We won't move you to

a safe house yet. But, if at any point I change my mind, you will go. If you like it, or not. In the meantime, you will follow all of my instructions."

She nodded. "Of course. I wouldn't do anything to put Kayla in further danger."

Sawyer wasn't too sure about that. But at the moment, it seemed easier not to fight her and Deputy Director Williams.

Deputy Director Williams clapped him on the back. "Good. I'm glad you're seeing reason. Now tell me. Are you sure you want to be part of this case? I can get someone else in here to help Agent Anderson, if you'd prefer."

"That won't be necessary." The muscle in his jaw twitched. "Like you pointed out, we don't want to upset the killer by changing any of his plans. Besides, I owe it to Agent Miller to see this through to the end. I'm going to make this creep pay for his crimes."

Hoyt rejoined the group. "NYPD officers are at your sister's apartment. They've spoken with her roommate."

"That would be Kayla's best friend, Monica Yothers." The worried expression etched on the rookie's face gave Sawyer cause for concern. "What aren't you telling me?"

"Your sister's roommate told the police that

Kayla left New York on the eleventh. Headed to Barton Creek."

"That doesn't make sense. Kayla would have told me she was coming."

"According to Ms. Yothers, the decision to visit you was prompted by events that occurred on the tenth."

Sawyer was half of a second away from strangling the younger man. "Spit. It. Out," he said through gritted teeth.

"It seems your sister became engaged, sir. She and her fiancé—a Mr. Jonathan Smith—were headed here to share the news with you."

"Then we have two missing people?" Bridget queried.

"We don't know if anyone's missing. According to Monica, Kayla and Jonathan planned to stop in North Carolina to share the news with his family before continuing to Barton Creek." Hoyt shrugged. "Maybe they're somewhere midroute?"

The rookie was obviously trying to offer encouragement, but Sawyer knew better than to hold out hope.

Lovelorn had his sister. Sawyer just had to figure out how to get her back.

He turned to Williams. "Sir, I need all the data we gathered on Lovelorn faxed here immediately. Even though he's moved outside his preferred region, as long as we do nothing to upset him, he won't change his routine. If he says Kayla won't die until midnight on the twenty-third, his need to control the order of events won't allow him to change his plan. And that's going to work to our advantage."

Sawyer hoped he sounded more confident than he felt.

If he were being totally honest with himself, Sawyer doubted Lovelorn would stick to his original plan even if they followed his every command. To his knowledge, Lovelorn had never targeted two women at once, nor had he ever leaked the identities of his targets to the FBI prior to their deaths. When a killer changed his MO, nothing was guaranteed.

FOUR

Bridget opened her eyes and stretched. It took a moment for her brain to process the sight before her.

Her grandparents' dining room looked like a scene out of one of those television crime dramas. There were maps and charts along one wall. Someone had even brought in a large dry-erase board attached to a wooden easel on wheels. The table was littered with notepads, ink pens, markers, coffee cups and paper plates with remnants of sandwiches and doughnuts. She'd never seen anything like it. At Protective Instincts, her job was to guard clients by taking preventive security measures. She'd never hunted a criminal.

Tension and adrenaline bounced off the men in the room. Hoyt sat at the far end of the table tapping keys on a laptop, and Sawyer sat, hunched over a notepad, at the end of the table closest to her. Stubble cast a shadow on the profiler's chiseled jawline, and dark circles smudged the skin under his eyes. Apprehension knotted in her stomach. The relaxed, cheerful foreman had morphed into a tense, no-nonsense law enforcement officer.

Bridget sat on an oversize chair in the alcove where she'd positioned herself earlier while trying to be invisible—her feet tucked underneath her, one elbow propped on the arm of the chair, with her chin resting in her hand and her fingers pressed against her mouth to keep herself from speaking out. Unfortunately, she'd gotten too comfortable and fallen asleep.

She was awake now. As long as she stayed quiet and out of the way, neither Sawyer nor Hoyt would try to send her away from the action. Bridget had learned a long time ago that her petite size sometimes caused people to not take her seriously. Today, she would use her size to her advantage and hide in plain sight. She wanted—no, she needed—to be informed about what was happening.

Bridget craned her neck and eyed the antique clock mounted on the wall above the mantel. One fifteen. She'd lost two hours of valuable time. Desperate to catch up, she skimmed the dry-erase board.

Facts about the serial killer were listed in

bold, black, handwritten print. The handwriting was too neat to be Hoyt's. Sawyer's? The controlled, precise strokes suited his personality.

First known murder five years ago.

Number of victims increased by one each year: one the first, two the second, etc.

FBI foiled plans to kill target Mary Kate Newman.

Agent Miller became victim number ten.

Lovelorn assumed dead for the past eighteen months.

On and on the list continued, along with two photos of each of the women—one before they were murdered and one after. In each after photo, the victims were all dressed like Isabella had been. White lacy dress. A wreath of roses on their head.

Sawyer tapped the notepad he'd been writing on. "Did Monica find a photo yet? Surely someone took a picture of my sister and her fiancé at some point in the past six months. How about on social media? Who's checking that?"

"I'm searching now, sir." Hoyt's fingers flew over the keyboard.

"What about Jonathan's car? Do we have a description for the APB?"

"Monica said Jonathan doesn't own a car,

which isn't unusual in New York City. She said he surprised Kayla with tickets for a train trip after she accepted his proposal."

"Get Monica on the phone. Let me hear this from her instead of secondhand," Sawyer commanded as he pushed to his feet and started pacing.

Agent Anderson, who'd been standing in the doorway talking on his cell phone, spoke up. "Monica is working with a sketch artist to get a composite of Jonathan. Agent Hooper— the field agent from the NYC office—said he'd call when they finished."

"What's taking so long? Don't these people know my sister's life is in danger?"

Sawyer slammed his fist on the oak table, not three feet from where Bridget sat. She jumped. Biting her lip to keep from making a sound, she prayed they hadn't noticed she was awake. One. Two. Three seconds passed. She breathed. Sawyer hadn't seen her movement.

Had he gotten any rest? Probably not. Deputy Director Williams left hours earlier, leaving Agent Anderson and Sawyer in charge of the operation.

She questioned the wisdom of the deputy's decision, but the man was probably saving himself grief in the long run by keeping Sawyer working within the guidelines of the investigation. After watching Sawyer's type A personality in action this past week, Bridget knew he'd never be able to sit back and let someone else take charge. Not with his sister in danger. And not with his history with Lovelorn.

"Remember what you told me about going off half-cocked," Bridget said. "You won't do Kayla any good if you rush through this investigation without taking time to look at all the facts."

All eyes turned in her direction. She'd blown her cover, but so be it. What was she supposed to do, sit back and let Sawyer's emotions overrule his thinking? Her life was in jeopardy, just like his sister's, and she had watched as much of this exchange in silence as she intended to.

Sawyer turned toward her. "I thought you were sleeping."

"Yeah, I gathered as much. Of course, if I had been, your outburst would have awakened me. Now, why don't you catch me up to speed. Sometimes it helps to have someone who hasn't been over the material a thousand times offer a fresh perspective."

Bridget looked at Hoyt. With a nod, she indicated he should leave them alone. When her brother seemed to be gearing up to argue, she gave him one of her "don't mess with me" looks. Hoyt narrowed his eyes as if he were going to argue, but then stood and left the room. Agent Anderson looked from Bridget to Sawyer and followed her brother out of the room.

"I knew Kayla had met someone. She said they met at the coffee shop where she works part-time. Jonathan's some kind of computer guru. He travels all the time, gone to a new location almost weekly." Sawyer raked his hand through his hair. "With their busy schedules, I figured they were years away from an engagement."

She nodded. What could she say? She'd never been an expert on love, or how long it took to know if someone was *the one*. The only man she'd dated for more than a year made a swift exit from her life after seeing her scars and hearing the doctor's prognosis of her inability to bear children.

"What kind of big brother am I? I've never even met the man my sister's going to marry." He sank into a chair. "She could be dead."

As much as this man's arrogant demeanor could infuriate her, she'd much rather deal with that attitude than this one. She suspected frustration and exhaustion prompted his display of vulnerability.

"She's not dead. You know this. You know Lovelorn's MO."

"Do I? At one time, I thought I did. Then I messed up. An agent lost her life, because of me."

"No. Not because of you. Because of Lovelorn. He's the killer, not you." She softened her tone. "You made a mistake, but mistakes don't define who we are. Especially when we learn lessons from them."

He studied his hands, refusing to look at her. "How can I guarantee I won't mess up this time?"

"You can't. All you can do is trust your gut. From what I heard earlier when the deputy director was talking to Agent Anderson, you're very good at controlling your emotions and looking at the facts." Bridget walked over to Sawyer and sat beside him. "You can't treat this any differently than you would any other case."

"He has my sister. I can't let her down."

Did she imagine it, or had he whispered "Not again"?

"The only way not to let her down is to treat this like any other case."

"How did you get to be so wise?" Sawyer asked, finally looking at her.

"Oh, I don't know. Years of experience?" She smiled, hoping he didn't catch the slight tremble in her voice. If only he knew all that she'd been through to bring her to this point of wisdom. And how truly unsure of herself she was. "So what's our next move?"

"Moving you to a safe house," he replied, his face impassable.

"Now wait a minute. I'm as much a part of this—"

"Sawyer's right, Munchkin."

Bridget looked up to see her brother Ryan standing in the doorway, Hoyt a shadow behind him.

"Ryan!" She rushed to hug him. "How did you get here so quickly?"

"You seem to forget my partner has friends in high places. Linc called in a favor and arranged a private jet to fetch me home." He pulled back and smiled down at her. "Looks like I got here just in time."

"Don't you start in on me, too. I'm not going anywhere. I'm done hiding." It had taken this incident to make her realize that she'd been hiding all these months since the attack. Not anymore. "It's time I start living again, and I don't know a better way to do that than to help save someone else's life."

Time I start living again. What had Bridget meant by that? Sawyer filed it away in his brain. Another question to ask in his quest to unravel the mysteries surrounding this intriguing woman. But not now. First, he planned to use the fiery redhead's brothers to help persuade her to see reason. Then, he planned to rescue his sister and put Lovelorn behind bars.

Sawyer followed as Ryan escorted Bridget down the hallway and into the living room. "Listen, Short—"

"No, I will not listen. Not as long as you all insist on calling me names."

"Calling you names? What are you talking about?"

"Peanut. Shorty. Munchkin. And about twenty other names that you've all called me through the years."

Hoyt snorted from the doorway, and Ryan shot him a look filled with daggers. "Don't you have work to do, little brother? Or does the FBI pay you to lurk in corners and eavesdrop?"

Sawyer smiled when Hoyt stepped outside his brother's view, but didn't go away as instructed.

Even though the siblings were being snippy with each other, Sawyer knew there was a lot of love in the room. A longing for lost moments washed over him. There was no way to change the past. His mother had robbed him and Kayla of having a close sibling relationship like the one playing out in front of him because she couldn't let go of emotional wounds inflicted by his father. Another reason Sawyer had never married. Too great a risk involved. He never wanted to go through life like his mother had, never healing from her broken heart. No, it was much better to live life alone.

"I know you guys don't mean anything by the nicknames, but I think you sometimes forget I'm a grown woman." The earnest plea in her voice tugged at Sawyer's heart. This dynamic woman had her own insecurities.

"I can hold my own in most situations. Well, until recently, that is. But I can't run and hide every time life gets tough." Bridget jutted out her chin and gave her big brother an I-dare-you-to-argue look.

"I know you're a grown woman, Pea—Bridge." Ryan held up both of his hands, palms outward, as if warding off an attack. "Bridget."

Her features softened and the right side of her mouth tilted upward in a half smile. "Bridge is fine."

Ryan took off his glasses and rubbed his eyes. Replacing the square, black frames, he gazed down at his sister and shrugged. "Okay.

Bridge. But even *grown women* need protection sometimes. I can't let you put yourself in danger."

She arched an eyebrow. "Isn't that what I do every day that I go to work? Put myself in danger to protect others? How is this any different?"

"This isn't at all like the cases you've worked," Ryan exploded, a red flush creeping up his neck. "In every one of those situations, I knew the risk before sending you in. Besides, Linc or I were always around to watch your back."

"Oh, is that right? Is that why I almost died? Because it was a cushy job and there wasn't any danger?"

Almost died. Bridget's words rang in Sawyer's ears. How could a brother hire his sister to work in a dangerous profession?

"I admit I messed up. That time. Which is another reason I need to protect you this time. Please, be sensible," Ryan said.

"I am being sensible, and I'll accept protection. Just not the kind you want me to have."

"What does that mean?"

"It means I won't allow my brothers to coddle me, and I won't hide away in fear. Deputy Director Williams has already given approval for me to be involved with this case. So we—

Protective Instincts along with the FBI—need to implement precautions for my safety. Ones that don't involve a safe house.

"Besides, why should I worry about my safety? All I have to do is send out an SOS alert and you'll swoop in to rescue me. Right?" Bridget wrapped her arms around Ryan. "My brothers are the best possible bodyguards I could have. That includes you, too, Hoyt."

Hoyt stepped back into view with a sheepish expression on his face, confirming Sawyer's hunch. Bridget had her brothers wrapped around her beautiful little finger. He'd get no help from them in making her see reason.

Sawyer's phone rang, causing three sets of eyes to turn on him. His face warmed at being caught eavesdropping, and he fumbled as he pulled his phone out of his pocket.

Turning his back to the trio, he glanced at the screen. The sheriff's number flashed. "Agent Eldridge here. What can I do for you, sir?"

"Sheriff Evans over in Greene County just called. The owner of a hostel along the Appalachian Trail—" The sound of papers being shuffled came across the line. "Daniel Kendrick discovered the body of a hiker in the laundry facility this morning. Female. Midtwenties. Strawberry blonde." With each new description, Sawyer's grip tightened on his phone. "White dress. Wreath of…"

"Pink and white roses," he said in unison with Sheriff Rice. A sinking feeling washed over him. Confident the killer only had his sights on Kayla and Bridget, Sawyer hadn't even considered that anyone else might be in danger. *I've messed up, again.*

"Yes, sir. Looks like your killer has struck again, son. Oh, and he left another note." Sawyer felt a tap on his shoulder and turned, making eye contact with questioning green eyes as the sheriff said, "This time it's addressed to Ms. Bridget Vincent."

Nervous energy zinged through Bridget as she leaned against the wooden railing on the wraparound porch that encircled the hostel. What was taking Sawyer so long? Processing a crime scene took time, but they'd been here for over two hours.

She looked off toward the horizon. The sun dipped lower in the sky, and rays of orange, red and gold peeked through the clouds as a misty fog danced in the valley. She shivered. Whether from nerves or the twenty-degree drop in temperature that blanketed the area shortly after their arrival, Bridget did not know.

She was ready to get a look at the letter the killer left for her. Though she wished he'd stop using dead bodies as his means of delivery. Sawyer said Lovelorn was playing games with them. This seemed to be a fair assessment. Too bad she'd never enjoyed playing games, especially when other people knew the rules and she didn't.

"Munchkin… I mean Bridge. Stop bouncing. Please."

At Ryan's command, her leg stilled. Bridget hadn't even been aware of her movements. She shrugged. "I'm sorry. Guess you can tell I'm anxious."

A smile lifted the corners of Ryan's mouth before he looked back down at his scuff-toed boots and kicked a twig off the corner of the porch. His nonchalant attitude didn't faze her a bit. It was, in fact, a standard response from the brother who refused to let little things get to him.

"What do you think is in the letter?" she asked, praying he could offer words of encouragement to quell the butterflies in her stomach.

"I really wouldn't know." He looked toward the group of investigators standing near the edge of the property, urging the hikers to continue along the trail.

"Nothing to see here," they said. "Move along" and "No one can stay in the hostel tonight" became the officers' mantra.

Bridget searched for Sawyer and found him standing on the other side of the long porch talking to a tall, lanky blond-haired man who looked like he'd be as much at home on a beach somewhere as he appeared to be here in the mountains.

"Do you think that's the person who found the body? He seems awfully young to be the owner of a hostel."

"That's him all right. I asked one of the Greene County deputies about him. Name's Daniel Kendrick. Thirty-five years old. Has an engineering degree. Walked away from the stress of his high-powered job and took over the family business when his parents retired and moved to Florida last year."

According to the brochure Bridget picked up when they arrived, the family business, located fifty feet off the trail in a small mountain town with a population of less than five hundred, seemed to be thriving. There were six cabins on the property—a small cabin that housed the office, three family cabins that would each sleep up to eight people, a bathhouse with six separate showering rooms for hikers who didn't want to stay the night but wanted a chance to clean up, and the hostel, a large cabin with dorm-style sleeping quarters that would accommodate twenty and held a communal living space that included four bathrooms, a kitchen and a laundry room.

The section of town that Bridget could see from her vantage point consisted of a general grocery, a post office and a diner.

For the hundredth time, she wondered what could be taking so long. Sawyer and Daniel seemed to be in deep conversation. Then the hostel owner went into the main office area and returned a few seconds later with a key that he handed to Sawyer. What was that all about?

"Look, Bridge, we've been here too long. And you really shouldn't be out here. It's too wide open. Let me take you back to the ranch." Ryan pushed off the rail and turned to face her, blocking her view of the men and causing her to twist to see around him. "Sawyer can bring the evidence when—"

A gunshot rang out.

Ryan's face contorted in pain as the sleeve of his crisp white button-down was washed in red. Blood.

"Ryan!" His name came out in a strangled cry.

He pushed her to the hard wooden deck,

covering her as a torrent of gunfire sounded around them.

"I'm fine. Stay down," Ryan rasped, his breathing labored.

The gunfire ceased and Ryan's body went limp, his one-hundred-and-seventy-pound frame effectively pinning her to the ground. Bridget heard the faint sound of an engine, followed by muffled shouts. Though she could not make out what was being said, she knew the law enforcement officers on-site were scrambling to apprehend the sniper. Had anyone even seen Ryan get shot?

She struggled to force air into her lungs, and the pounding in her ears grew louder. No. Not pounding. Footsteps. Running toward them. *Lord, please let it be friend and not foe approaching.* If only she could twist her head to look.

"Bridget. Are you okay?"

Sawyer. Relief washed over her even as the weight of her brother bore down on her.

"Ryan's been shot. Help me. Get him off."

"Hang on." His voice faded, and Bridget suspected he called over his shoulder for assistance. "Help me move him off her. But be careful. We won't know how serious the wound is until we remove his shirt."

"Let me spread this blanket out." Bridget

didn't recognize the voice. Maybe it was one of the county deputies. But what about the shooter? Was it Lovelorn? Had they apprehended him?

She felt light-headed, so she focused on trying to take shallow, controlled breaths.

"Okay. Ready. Go." At Sawyer's command, Ryan's body was lifted and air rushed into Bridget's lungs. She took in two deep gulps, then rolled over and crawled the few feet to her brother.

The dark gray blanket under him seemed to pull the remaining color from his pallid face.

Bridget tried to rip her brother's shirt open, but the fabric and buttons held. Her fingers shook as she tried again, and failed. "Ugh. Why can't I get this open?"

"Let me do that." The hostel owner flipped open a pocketknife, and after Sawyer pulled her back a few inches, he slid the blade under the cuff of the sleeve and sliced the material open all the way to the shoulder.

The bullet had hit high on Ryan's bicep. Blood poured out of the wound. Bridget blanched. *Please, Lord, don't let him die.* A sense of helplessness washed over her. Was this how her family felt the night Robert attacked her?

"Help me." Sawyer knelt beside her and

slid his hands under Ryan's neck and shoulder. "I'm going to lift him about six inches off the ground. I want you to finish ripping the sleeve off. We'll use it to make a tourniquet to control the bleeding."

"Isn't that dangerous? I read that the use of a tourniquet could cause the loss of the limb." She hated to question Sawyer. At least he had a plan and seemed to know more about trauma care than she did.

"Only if it's left on too long. He's losing too much blood. We need to get this done now." Hazel eyes met hers. "Ready?"

She nodded, her throat too dry for words. He gave her a half smile. "Okay. Go!"

When Sawyer lifted him, Ryan's face contorted, and he opened his eyes, spurring her into action. Her heart thundered against her chest, and her hands shook, making her feel clumsy and slow.

"Lift…higher," Ryan managed to say, pushing against the ground with his good arm. Sawyer helped him to a seated position as the sleeve broke free.

She tied the tourniquet as high as she could above the wound. "Has anyone called an ambulance?"

"I did. ETA ten minutes. I'll go to the road

to watch for them." Daniel hurried toward the drive.

Ryan moaned, and Sawyer helped him ease back onto the blanket.

Bridget brushed her brother's hair back as tears ran down her face. "It's okay, Ryan. You're going to be fine. It's my fault you got shot. I'm so sorry."

"It's not your...fault. Besides." He gave her a weak smile. "This is just a flesh wound."

"That's not a flesh wound. Even if it was, flesh wounds don't make you pass out."

"I didn't...pass out. I was just light-headed and...couldn't move... That's all."

Her big brother was putting on a tough-guy act. He was going to be okay. Relief bubbled up and turned into a crying laughter. Bridget leaned over and kissed his forehead. "I love you, bro."

Straightening, she met Sawyer's eyes. "Where's the shooter?" she whispered. "Are we safe here?"

Sawyer nodded. "The shots came from the ridge. When we returned fire, the sniper took off on a four-wheeler."

The sound of a siren grew louder, and tires screeched as the ambulance turned into the driveway.

The emergency vehicle rolled to a stop

not more than ten feet from the edge of the porch. A paramedic jumped from it and rushed toward them, carrying a red medic bag. "What've we got?"

"Gunshot wound. Right shoulder. Hit from behind. Clear exit. Tourniquet has slowed but not stopped the bleeding." Sawyer's clipped response emphasized the urgency of the situation.

Sawyer stood and pulled Bridget to her feet. "Come on. Let's give them room to work."

"I need to stay here." She tried to fight against him.

"No. The medics need room to work. And we've gotta talk." He searched the area. "Somewhere private and protected."

He pulled her down the steps, passing Daniel and a second medic carrying a stretcher onto the porch. Bridget allowed Sawyer to guide her to the back of the ambulance. Its open doors offered protection from every side but one. Adrenaline had kept her going until that moment, but now reality hit like a sucker punch to the solar plexus. Lovelorn could get to her or a family member, anytime, anyplace.

FIVE

Sawyer fingered the plastic bag in his pocket. How could he share the letter with Bridget now? She'd want to go with her brother to the hospital. He couldn't blame her. But if she left, he'd never see his sister again. At least not alive.

"What was so urgent you couldn't let me stay with Ryan?" Worry was etched on Bridget's face, and he read concern mingled with fear in her eyes.

He swallowed. "It's just that. Look, Bridget, Ryan's going to be okay. I've seen wounds like this before. They look much worse than they really are."

"Is that a fact? It's comforting to know that you're an expert on bullet wounds just like you're an expert on ever—" Her eyes rounded, and she bit her lower lip.

A blush swept up her face, and Sawyer recalled her earlier comments about needing to learn to control her tongue. Knowing she regretted saying the things she'd said didn't take away the sting of her words.

"I wasn't trying to pretend to be an expert. I only wanted to offer encouragement." He turned toward the group of men tending to Ryan. "If you feel you need to be over there—in the way—by all means, don't let me stop you."

He heard her sigh.

"You sounded a lot like Ryan just then," she said. After a moment's hesitation, she added, "I'm sorry. You didn't drag me over here to discuss Ryan's condition. You might as well tell me what's on your mind. Is it about the letter Lovelorn left for me?"

At her question, he instinctively pulled the letter from his pocket. That's when he realized he had gotten blood on the evidence bag. Ryan's blood. How could he have been so careless?

Sawyer grunted. "Hang on."

He pushed the envelope back into his pocket, wiped his hands on his jeans in a futile effort to clean them, then climbed inside the ambulance, and pulled a pair of gloves out of the dispenser mounted to the wall.

He pushed his hands into the gloves before pulling out another pair and handing them to Bridget.

She took the offering, and Sawyer sat down on the floor of the vehicle and dangled his feet over the edge.

He looked over Bridget's shoulder. Officers from several agencies that had already been on scene were searching the woods for the shooter, but they wouldn't find him. Lovelorn was too cunning.

Looking toward Ryan, Sawyer noted the medics preparing to lift him onto the stretcher. "Looks like they've got him stable and ready for transport. We don't have long to decide."

"What kind of decision?"

"I need you to stay here. You can't go with Ryan to the hospital." Sawyer's voice sounded desperate even to his own ears.

"What? Have you lost your mind?" Her voice rose to a shrill pitch. "There's no way I'll abandon my brother like that."

"Right now, I need you more than your brother does. Ryan is receiving the proper care. He'll be fine. I promise." *Lord, don't let my promise be a lie.*

Sawyer met her eyes without blinking. He hated to beg, but he would if that was what it took to get her to do as he asked.

"My sister is out there." He swept his hand toward the woody, mountain trail. "Somewhere. With a killer." Sawyer shoved his hand back into his pocket, fisted the letter and pulled it out a wrinkled mess. "In this letter, the killer vows to murder Kayla if we don't follow his instructions. Including us—you and me—being up by morning light, following the clues to a scavenger hunt he's laid out for us."

She took the letter from his grasp and stared at the envelope without opening it.

"All right, folks, we need y'all outta there. We've gotta get this guy loaded and headed toward the hospital."

Bridget jumped at the sound of the medic. "How's Ryan? Is he going to be okay?" Rushing to the stretcher, she clutched her brother's hand.

"I'm fine, Squirt. I mean—" Ryan coughed.

"Squirt's fine." She hiccupped, tears pooling in her eyes. She blinked them away as she addressed the ambulance driver. "Which hospital are you taking him to?"

"The closest one is Laughlin Memorial. Forty-five minutes away. But it'll take longer if you keep holding us up."

Sawyer grasped Bridget's shoulders and, for the second time that evening, pulled her away from her brother's side. Why did his sister's safety have to depend on Bridget being here when she needed to be with Ryan? His chest tightened. "Let's call Hoyt. He can meet the ambulance at the hospital." His voice came out gruffer than intended.

She looked from Ryan back to Sawyer. Was she wavering? "No. I want to go with my brother. Don't you see he needs me?" She pulled on the door and reached up to climb in ahead of the attendant.

Defeated, Sawyer let go of her sleeve, his hand dropping to his side. He'd failed. Again.

The stretcher brushed his leg, and he looked down, making eye contact with Ryan. Bridget's brother held up his uninjured arm. "Hang on, guys. I need a moment." Ryan searched Sawyer's face. "You can't do this without her, can you?"

"No," Sawyer answered grimly, with a shake of his head.

"That's what I was afraid of." Ryan motioned for the medics to continue, and Sawyer stepped back to give them room.

Once they were loaded, the medics moved about, securing things while Bridget and Ryan talked in hushed tones. Sawyer turned to leave. He needed to call Agent Anderson to see if he and Hoyt had uncovered any additional evidence while Sawyer had been away. As he reached for his phone, it dinged.

He pulled the cell out of his pocket. He'd received a text from Hoyt.

Sheriff Rice called. On my way. Will meet ambulance at hospital. Also, background check came back. Your sister is marrying an upstanding citizen who appears to have social media phobia. Still searching for a picture.

The ambulance roared to life. Sawyer turned to watch his only hope of saving his sister leave in a cloud of dust and came face-to-face with an auburn-haired beauty, a solemn expression on her face.

"I thought you'd left." He could have kicked himself. It sounded so cliché, like something from an old black-and-white movie. He stepped toward her and tried again. "I know it was hard for you to stay behind. Thank you."

She didn't move. "Ryan said to tell you he isn't willing to sacrifice his sister for yours. If anything happens to me, there won't be any place on this earth you can hide and be safe from my brothers."

A chill crawled up Sawyer's spine. He didn't doubt her words one bit. But he refused to worry about her brother's threats, because he had no intentions of letting either woman lose her life.

* * *

Even though she already had the words memorized, Bridget picked up the evidence bag that held the note and read it through the clear plastic.

Our paths crossed inadvertently.
Now, your death is a certainty.
Kayla's set to be my next bride.
Will you save her or run and hide?
I hope you will stay and play my game.
No matter, the end result will be the same.

Bridget had always dreamed of a man writing poetry for her. Too bad, when it finally happened, the guy had to be a sadistic serial killer who wanted to make her one of his victims.

"So, you mean to tell me we're going on a scavenger hunt, following clues set out by a killer?" Bridget knew her voice had accelerated several octaves, but she didn't care. "How can we be sure Lovelorn won't be hiding somewhere waiting to jump us?"

"We can't. But I don't think he would have gone to so much trouble to plan a scavenger hunt if he didn't intend on us reaching the end. He wants us to play this his way, and he isn't likely to stop the game until we reach the goal."

"You truly expect me to follow you blindly along the Appalachian Trail?"

"Lots of women hike the AT. You'll be fine. Daniel has all the gear you'll need." Sawyer looked to the young hostel owner, who had been gracious enough to let them use his personal cabin for this discussion. "His mom left clothes, shoes and camping gear behind when she moved to Florida."

"Yeah. Although you're shorter than my mom, but I'm sure we can find something that'll work." Daniel pulled a box out of the closet in the entryway. "What size shoe do you wear?"

"Seven." Why was she answering his questions? This was ridiculous. She couldn't go on this hike, and it wasn't because she was a woman. Bridget had always been athletic, but her body wasn't completely healed from the attack and subsequent surgeries. Though Sawyer didn't know about that.

He also didn't know hiking trails made her feel vulnerable, with no way of knowing who or what was waiting around the next bend in the trail looking for an opportunity to attack.

Her heart raced, her skin hot and clammy.

"Um. If you'll excuse me, I think I'll step outside and call the hospital to check on Ryan."

"Hoyt promised to call if there's any change." Sawyer looked up from the crudely drawn map Lovelorn included with the letter.

"It's been hours. I need an update." She stood to leave, and he put a restraining hand on her arm.

"It's been less than an hour. But I understand. Stay here and make your phone call. I don't want you outside by yourself. Daniel and I will leave so you can have privacy."

She laughed. "You seem to forget there are still police officers and federal investigators swarming the property trying to find the shooter. I think I'll be safe."

"Still." He smiled, slid his hand down her arm, clasped her hand and squeezed, leaving a trail of goose bumps. "I'd rather not take a chance of having to spend the rest of my life running from your brothers."

Sawyer winked, let go of her hand and turned toward the door that separated the living quarters from the main office. "Daniel, why don't you leave that box. Bridget can go through it once she gets off the phone. In the meantime, you and I will go look over the large map you have hanging in the office.

We'll see if we can match up this drawing to any part of the map."

As soon as the two men left, Bridget pulled out her phone and called Hoyt. The call went straight to his voice mail. Frustrated, she hung up and called Protective Instincts.

Amelia, the motherly office manager, answered on the first ring. "Bridget. Are you okay?"

"I'm fine. I was wondering if you'd heard anything from Hoyt. He's not answering his phone."

"He called Lincoln about forty-five minutes ago. Said the surgery went well, and Ryan's in stable condition. Didn't he call you?"

"He did. I just wanted an update. It's hard being here and not at the hospital." She fingered the seams on the sofa as she spoke, absentmindedly tracing the pattern.

"Why aren't you at the hospital? I can't imagine anything keeping you away from one of your brothers when they're in need."

"You already know why. I'm sure Ryan and Hoyt have filled Linc in on what's going on around here. And we both know if anyone at PI knows something you want to know, you have ways of finding out."

"You exaggerate." Melodious laughter came across the line, but then dropped off abruptly. "Okay, I know a serial killer has threatened you. What I don't understand is why you're not at a safe house somewhere. Why don't you let me book you on the next flight to Denver. You can stay with me until they catch this guy."

Her heart swelled with love. She couldn't keep letting her family and friends rush to her rescue and putting them in danger. Bridget had to see this through to the end, no matter how many fears she had to face.

"I appreciate the offer, but I'm needed here. Listen, I've gotta go. I'll talk to you later." Bridget hung up before Amelia could try to persuade her to change her mind.

After sliding the phone into her pocket, Bridget dragged the cardboard box over to the couch so she could go through its contents.

Who was she kidding? She'd known she was going on this scavenger hunt from the moment she stepped out of the ambulance, allowing her brother to be sprinted off to the hospital without her.

All she could do now was pray she could outsmart the madman who'd decided to use her as a pawn in his real-life game of chance. Last time, she had been attacked without warning. This time, she'd be on guard, and she would not go down without a fight.

SIX

"Remind me again why we had to leave before the rooster crowed." Bridget tried to shift the weight of the backpack to alleviate some of the pressure of the shoulder straps bearing down on her scars.

Sawyer kept a steady pace, leading the way into the dark, misty morning, unaware of Bridget's struggles. "You already know the answer."

Yes. She knew the answer. The clock was ticking. If they hoped to find Kayla before midnight Tuesday, they had to get moving. She'd memorized the note Lovelorn left on the back of the map that was now tucked securely in the side pocket on the waist belt of Sawyer's backpack.

Kayla is hidden off the beaten track.
Follow the map if you hope to get her back.
Her fiancé won't be as easy to discover,

Since I left him hidden under cover.
If I see any law enforcement on the trail,
You'll get another letter by body mail.

After providing them with gear and food supplies, Daniel had given Bridget and Sawyer the use of the cabin located closest to the trail. They'd eaten sandwiches and then gone to their separate bedrooms to retire early. She hoped Sawyer had slept better than she had. Bridget had spent the night tossing and turning. When she'd finally fallen asleep, she had awakened in a cold sweat less than two hours later, after a nightmare of being chased through the woods by a man without a face. Then, she'd remained wide awake until Sawyer knocked on her door, letting her know it was time to get up and slip into the dark night.

They rounded a curve in the trail just as fingers of pink and gold sunlight inched above low-hanging clouds. Bridget had always been an early riser and would've loved to have watched this sunrise from the back porch of her grandparents' home with a cup of coffee and her Bible. She enjoyed starting her day reading from God's word, surrounded by His beauty. Now, two mornings in a row, the sunrises she loved so much had been marred by evil.

"What makes you think Agent Anderson and Hoyt aren't already at the hostel gearing up to follow us? I mean seriously, if they come tromping along the trail, it's just going to make our pen pal have a reason to deliver another letter." She shivered at the thought. "How do we stop that from happening?"

Sawyer's long strides halted, and in one swift move, he turned to face her. Bridget, unable to stop as abruptly, ran face-first into his chest. She bounced backward and would have toppled to the ground from the weight of her pack if not for the profiler's quick reflexes. Hands like branding irons fastened to her upper arms, keeping her from falling.

Sawyer bent at the waist, bringing his face even with hers. Nose to nose. Eye to eye. "Do you trust me?"

Whatever she'd expected him to say, it hadn't been that. Did she trust him? Yes. No. Maybe.

Would she be out here in the middle of the woods if she didn't trust him?

"Is that a no? You don't trust me." He dropped his hands from her arms, turned and paced a few steps ahead, then swung back to face her again.

She stood rooted into place, anticipating his next question.

"Why wouldn't you trust me?"

Bridget swallowed in an attempt to alleviate her parched throat. "You keep too many secrets."

"What? Are you kidding? I've bared my soul to you. Do you have any clue how hard it was for me to ask you to go along with this plan?"

"First, that is not baring your soul. And second, you didn't ask. It was more like an order. You told me I couldn't go with Ryan. You needed me."

A fallen log lay a few yards off the path, so Bridget waded through the underbrush toward it. They'd only been on the trail a couple of hours, but the straps of the backpack bit into her shoulders and her feet ached.

She released the clasp on the sternum strap but struggled with the one on the waist strap. Sawyer's hand slid around her waist, and with a click, she was free. Then he lifted the backpack off her shoulders and placed it on the ground.

"You're right. I didn't ask."

Bridget turned to look at Sawyer. And waited for him to continue.

He shrugged. "I have a need to control situations. I'm sorry."

Easing into a seated position on the log, she

stretched her sore muscles, making him wait for her response. Once she felt some sensation returning to her achy body, she replied, "I won't say it's okay, because it's not. I understand you're under pressure to save your sister and any other woman who may become prey to Lovelorn. But the only way we can successfully complete this mission is if we're totally honest with each other." Well, at least with things relevant to the hunt.

His backpack joined hers on the ground. Then he bent to dig around inside the front pocket, pulling out two protein bars before snatching the water bottles out of the side pockets of each pack.

"Here." He held out his hand, offering her the food and drink.

She reached for the water but ignored the protein bar. "Thanks. I'm not hungry."

"Doesn't matter. You need to eat." He extended his hand farther. "This is a grueling hike. I can't have you weak from hunger."

She accepted the offering, peeled the wrapper and took a bite of the bar. Fruit and nuts, a little chewy, but edible.

They ate in silence.

Bridget popped the last bite into her mouth, chewed and swallowed. "Thank you. I guess I was hungrier than I realized."

She took a swig of water and then placed the bottle along with the wrapper into her pack. Then she sat back, her hands folded in her lap, and absentmindedly twisted the ring she wore.

"Pretty ring."

"Huh?"

Sawyer looked pointedly at her hands. "The ring is pretty. It looks expensive. You probably should have left it behind. If you lose it, I'm sure it will upset your boyfriend."

Bridget glanced down at the beautiful emerald ring that graced the third finger of her right hand. Was it expensive? She'd never asked, though she was sure Ryan had ordered the jeweler to use only the best materials. The ring had to look authentic to hide its true purpose. Keeping her safe. With the flip of a tiny switch under the stone, Ryan would receive a notification on his phone, giving him her location. It was his way of trying to protect her from future attacks. Bridget had never activated the switch. Should she, now? No. Lovelorn's poem had said they would find Kayla *off the beaten track*. Which most likely meant he would send them on a side trail that was less traveled, making it easier for him to spot anyone trailing them. If one of her brothers got anxious and started following them, it could mean doom for them all. She'd hold off on sending an SOS signal, for now.

"I don't go anywhere without this ring, and I don't plan to lose it." With a sigh, she stood and hefted the backpack onto her back. "Also, for the record, it isn't from a boyfriend."

When he didn't say anything, she added, "What are we waiting for? Let's go."

He stood, his gaze locked on hers, probing. Was he using his profiling skills on her?

She ducked her head and adjusted the waist strap higher on her abdomen to allow the shoulder straps to hover above her shoulders and not actually touch them. Bridget wasn't sure how comfortable the alteration would be, but she had to alleviate the pain. If it didn't work, she'd try something else. Either way, she had come too far to give up now.

Looking up, it startled her to find Sawyer still assessing her movements. He opened his mouth to speak, probably to correct the way she'd fastened the pack, but apparently thought better of it. Instead, he closed his mouth and gave a slight shake of his head.

She bent to pick up his pack, intending to hand it to him. Why was it so heavy? If she had to guess, she'd say his backpack weighed more than twice as much as hers. "What do—"

"Here. Let me." He plucked the pack out of her hands and quickly fastened it into place.

"We need to get moving. Unless. You want to go back?"

"No. I don't want to go back." Bridget puffed out a breath. "I want to be treated like a partner. I may be a petite girl, but I grew up in this region. This will be a treacherous journey, especially if we're going off trail. We'll have to rely on each other to survive."

"Fair enough. I'll answer all of your questions as we walk."

"Thank you." She started back toward the trail, stopped and faced Sawyer. "Just so you know, I trust you. I wouldn't be here otherwise."

The statement earned her a smile that lit up his eyes. With the early morning lighting combined with the setting, Sawyer looked like a model who had stepped out of the pages of a camping magazine.

Bridget's breath caught, and her chest tightened. She closed her eyes. *Dear Heavenly Father, help my mind stay strong enough to overrule my heart. Don't let me long for things I can't have. No man deserves to be saddled with a woman like me. A woman with scars, both physical and emotional, that will never completely heal.*

Sawyer never knew three little words could hold so much power. When Bridget said "I trust you," his shoulders relaxed and a small portion of the tension that had taken up residence when he read Lovelorn's demands escaped in a tidal wave of relief.

He could do this. No. They could do this. But only if he learned how to relinquish some control. Was that even possible? Sawyer wasn't sure, but he'd have to try. Together, as a team, they could rescue his sister and keep themselves alive, too. Working against each other, or out of sync, would be disastrous.

"You never told me why you think Hoyt and Agent Anderson aren't already on the trail following us." Bridget's voice broke through his thoughts.

"Ryan overheard our conversation before they transported him to the hospital."

"Yeah, I know. That's why he encouraged me to stay behind. I think he figured this is our only hope to prevent Lovelorn from killing me and Kayla, and any other woman of his choosing."

"Right. When I checked with the hospital last, the nurse said Ryan was awake and his brother was with him."

"You checked on Ryan, again? After I went to bed?" Her face scrunched, as though she were deep in thought. "I guess that makes sense. You are the lead investigator on this case."

"I'm sure Ryan has filled Hoyt in by now." He continued as if she hadn't spoken. Bridget didn't need to know he'd checked on Ryan because he'd wanted to take her on the scavenger hunt without the added guilt of taking her away from a brother who needed her, and not because it was his job. "I also called Anderson and clued him in. He wasn't happy that we were going on the hunt without him."

"I'm kind of surprised he didn't show up at the cabin first thing this morning with agents in hiking gear set to go with us."

"I'm sure he did. Actually, he ordered us to stay put until he arrived this morning and assessed the situation."

"What?" Bridget gasped, coming to a standstill. "You disobeyed a direct command from your superior?"

"Depends on how you look at it." Sawyer shrugged. "I'm on a leave of absence, which means I'm not currently on the Bureau's payroll."

"And you think going rogue is the answer?"

"I don't consider this *going rogue*. I brought a satellite phone. We'll check in as often as possible with updates." He shoved his hand through his hair. "And I left copies of everything—the letter to you, the map and the poem—in an envelope addressed to Agent

Anderson, with instructions for Daniel to give it to him the moment he arrives. This way, Anderson and Hoyt will know where we've gone. They'll also understand trying to intervene will mean death for Kayla. And us."

She smiled and nodded. "Okay, if we're going to do this, we need to find our next clue."

They continued on their hike and soon reached a section of trail where a large fallen tree blocked their path. Sawyer climbed over it and extended a hand to help Bridget across.

The moment she placed her hand into his outstretched one, the desire to carry her as far away as possible washed over him. Sawyer had to protect her from the evil he'd brought into her life. Using Bridget as bait to save his sister, was he any better than Lovelorn? Bile rose in his throat, and he fought a wave of nausea.

Hastily, he turned back to the trail and tried to get his bearings. Fog engulfed the area, and even though it was daylight now, it was impossible to see more than three feet in any direction.

"What happens when we reach our destination?"

There was no easy way to say this, so he was blunt. "Lovelorn will try to kill us. All of us."

He felt a tug on his backpack and turned to find Bridget with a scowl on her face. "I'm not stupid or naive. Regardless of what Lovelorn has said, I know he plans to kill *all* of us. I want to know what your plan is to keep that from happening."

"My plan is to follow the clues and see where they lead me. As we get closer to the spot where he's holding Kayla, I'll find a place where we can hide so we can observe the situation and develop a course of action."

Reaching into the side pocket of his pack, he pulled out the map and flicked the crumpled paper open. Time to check their route.

They hadn't met any hikers yet, and he prayed they wouldn't. Another reason he'd insisted they leave in the middle of the night to start their journey, though he'd known the hiking would be dangerous and slow with headlamps for their only light.

"Lovelorn marked a spot on the map where we're to get off the path. This drawing looks like a tipi with a double white blaze mark painted above it. A double white blaze tells hikers—"

"There's an obscure turn, route change or incoming side trail," Bridget rattled off like a trail guide.

He raised an eyebrow. "Exactly."

The pixie smiled impishly and pulled the map down where she could get a better view. "This isn't a tipi. It's a tree with a hollowed-out trunk. I remember the first time I saw it. I think I was eight or nine." Bridget's features softened, and her expression took on a faraway look. "Dad was taking Charlie, Nate and Ryan hiking and camping for a weekend. I begged to go. The boys didn't want me to tag along. Of course, who could blame teenage boys for not wanting their kid sister around? Dad compromised. He told the boys if they'd let me go for one night, he'd have Mom pick me up the next day, and they could extend their hike for an extra couple of days."

A muscle in his jaw twitched.

"You've been on this trail before?" Good. His voice sounded controlled, even though it upset him she'd kept this from him. "Why didn't you mention this earlier?"

"Because when I expressed concern, you said, and I quote, 'Lots of women hike the AT. You'll be fine.' You automatically assumed that I'm a frail woman consumed with fear of the unknown." She shrugged. "Because of my size, I've spent my entire life trying to prove I'm not helpless. I refuse to do that anymore, so I let you think what you wanted."

"Bridget." He grasped her shoulders, and

she grimaced. Sawyer loosened his grip, remembering the way she'd adjusted the straps on her backpack earlier to lessen the weight on her shoulders. She was obviously in tremendous pain. He'd offer to carry her pack, but he sensed this wasn't the time. Maybe he could help her shift it so it didn't bear down on her. He started adjusting her straps as he continued, "I think you're many things, but frail isn't one of them. Talkative, stubborn, compassionate and fierce come to mind."

She reached up and stilled his hand. "Thank you. For fixing my pack, and for the compliments. At least that's the way I'm choosing to take your words. I guess I can't expect you to treat me as an equal and share everything you know if I'm not willing to do the same. I'm sorry." Her smile was enough to light up the forest.

If they'd met under different circumstances and he didn't know what love did to a person, he might find himself willing to... No. He couldn't let his mind go there. "Okay, so. Where's this tree?"

"Coming through." A voice sounded out of the fog, and they immediately stepped to the right of the trail.

A scruffy, bearded man with white hair and a raggedy Tilley broad-brim hat came into view. He carried a pack that seemed impossibly large for his slender frame. A black Lab followed at his heels with a small pack of his own. "Good morning, folks. Nice day for a walk."

"Yes, sir." Sawyer offered a polite response, intent on letting the man continue down the trail without holding him up. But Bridget had other ideas.

"Good morning, sir. What a beautiful dog. Have you been on the trail long?"

"Four and a half months. People on the trail call me Mountain Man, and this is Midnight." He rubbed a hand down the back of the dog's neck. "This is our third through-hike in the past eight years. We start near our home in Maine and work our way down to my daughter's house in north Georgia."

"Then you're familiar with the trail?"

"I'd like to think so."

"I wonder if you could tell me where the tree is that looks like a tipi." Her question caught Sawyer off guard, causing his breath to catch and sending him into a fit of coughing. Had she lost her mind? They didn't need a witness to their actions.

Bridget ignored him. "My daddy brought me on the trail for an overnight trip when I was young. He specifically started at a point that allowed us to pass that tree. I spent an hour playing and pretending to be Pocahontas before he insisted it was time to continue on our hike. I thought we might be close."

The elderly gentleman smiled and rubbed his chin, pulling on his whiskers. "The tree you're looking for is about a mile farther up trail. It's right before a bend in the trail. Can't miss it, has a trail blaze painted on it. Make sure to follow the trail carefully so you don't get lost. Though if you go off trail, won't take you long to figure out your error. You can turn around and backtrack."

"Thank you, sir. We'll be careful." Sawyer placed his hand on Bridget's back. They needed to get moving before they crossed paths with other innocent hikers. "Come on, dear, maybe we can take a few minutes to let you relive your childhood and still have time to make it to Allen Gap before we stop for the night."

Mountain Man laughed. "You've set a mighty goal, young man. Just remember, if you rush through life the way you plan to rush along this trail, you'll miss all of God's beauty. Not to mention, put yourself at risk of serious injuries." He tilted his hat at Bridget. "Good day, miss. Enjoy your hike."

They walked in silence until Sawyer was

sure they'd gone far enough along the trail to be out of Mountain Man's range of hearing.

Slowing his stride, he fell in step with Bridget and walked beside her. "What were you thinking back there? We don't need to involve innocent people in this."

"I was thinking we could use some guidance. If the fog doesn't clear, we'll have some idea of when we're getting close to our mark. Besides, he's headed in the opposite direction. It's not like he's going to see us go off trail and try to stop us."

Sawyer let her words sink in. Of course, she was right. Her interaction with Mountain Man had revealed important information and hadn't caused any harm. He needed to remember they were on the same side. She wouldn't do anything to jeopardize the mission.

The trail inclined and narrowed, so he moved back in front of her. To their left was a wall of rock, but to their right was a steep drop-off. He concentrated on putting one foot in front of the other, moving at a snail's pace, wishing the fog would lift. "Be careful to follow in my footsteps. You may even want to hang on to the back of my pack. I'd hate for you to fall off the side of the mountain."

Her laughter started softly and increased in

volume until he was sure everyone in a ten-mile radius could hear her. He dared not look back in case he missed his footing. "What's so funny?"

"You. If I hold on to your backpack, there's a greater risk that we'll both fall and never be found." She chortled. "Just keep moving. I'm fine."

Ten minutes later, the terrain leveled. Almost instantly, the fog lifted. The views were breathtaking. Too bad they didn't have time to enjoy the scenery. Continuing along the trail, they rounded a curve and the tipi tree stood before them. An image of a young Bridget with long, flowing red hair running in and out of the opening flashed before his eyes.

"It's the tree." She burst past him and ducked into the opening. Taking off her backpack, she plopped down, cross-legged, and faced him. "I think this is a good place for us to take a quick break and eat a snack before we continue. What do you think?"

What did he think? He thought she was the most beautiful woman he'd ever seen, and he wished he could stay here with her forever, sheltering her from all evil. Instead, he was leading her, like a lamb to slaughter, into the lair of a madman.

* * *

They ate in silence. Daniel had packed a mixture of protein bars, dried fruit, nuts, beef jerky and a few packages of MREs. She frowned. Meals ready to eat might be lifesavers for soldiers, but Bridget hoped she and Sawyer wouldn't get desperate enough to try them.

She took a sip of water. "Um, Sawyer? What are we going to do when we run out of water?"

"We'll have to locate a stream or waterfall, collect water and treat it with the tablets that Daniel sent with us."

"About that. How can we be sure Daniel isn't working with Lovelorn? What if he helped set this whole thing up? He could be poisoning us right this minute with tainted food." She felt ridiculous for not having questioned Daniel's help sooner. His build was similar to the man they'd seen in the pictures. Bridget gasped. "What if he's Lovelorn? He could have paid someone to fire that shot earlier!"

A smile spread across the handsome profiler's face. His eyes sparkled with suppressed laughter. "I called the Greene County sheriff on our way to the hostel, while you and Ryan were discussing all the reasons you should go into a safe house. The sheriff has known Daniel since he was a small child. Watched him grow up. Seems Daniel was a track star in high school and took his team to state."

"So you're going on the word of the sheriff? I'm sorry, but there have been many killers throughout history who no one suspected of being a murderer. And Daniel hasn't been here all of his life. What about when he was away at college or working as an engineer?"

"Believe me, I wish it were that easy to catch this guy. However, until last year, Daniel lived in California. Over two thousand miles from the murders. He's not our guy." Sawyer draped his arm across her shoulder. "And he's not an accomplice, either. Lovelorn works alone. Of that, I'm sure. He wouldn't have gotten this far if he didn't."

The warmth of his arm engulfed her like a hug on a snowy day. For a brief second, she allowed her mind and body to relax.

Blocking out the world and forgetting everything was impossible. Even if the threat from Lovelorn wasn't looming on the horizon, she couldn't allow herself to forget her inability to have children. *Every man wants a biological child.* Her ex's voice echoed inside her brain. Bridget shuddered.

"Are you cold? Daniel warned the temperatures would drop in the higher elevations. I have a parka in my pack. Let me get it." He dug into his backpack, but the cold she felt couldn't be chased away by adding another layer of clothing.

"No. I'm fine." She concentrated on gathering their trash. Bridget felt Sawyer's gaze boring into the back of her head, but she refused to look up and meet his eyes.

"Okay." He pulled the map out of his pack. "According to this, we're supposed to veer right. Looks like there's an outcropping of rocks right before the trail comes to a T. And close to the outcropping of rocks, he's drawn a...turtle?"

Following his finger, she looked at the drawing. It definitely looked like a turtle. "The tipi was really a tree, so I'd say there's a good chance the turtle isn't a real turtle."

Sawyer snagged her hand and pulled her to her feet. She stumbled and fell against his chest. Placing a hand under her chin, he tilted her head until her eyes met his. Was he going to kiss her? Did she want him to? Yes. That was a problem.

Taking a step backward, Bridget broke eye contact. She ducked out of the tree, her heart racing. "Let's find that next clue so we can catch this guy."

SEVEN

Two hours later, the sun bore down on them. Costa Del Mar sunglasses perched on her nose made Bridget happy she'd snagged her purse off the counter before leaving the ranch the day before. Even though he constantly touted being prepared, Sawyer hadn't had such foresight. Fortunately for him, she always carried a pair of cheap sunglasses in case she needed to provide a disguise for a client.

She bit back a laugh as she looked at his profile with the oversize women's glasses on his face. "I'm sorry I don't have better sunglasses for you to wear."

"If you were a compassionate person, you'd let me wear your Costas since they're gender neutral," he grumbled.

That did it. Laughter bubbled up from inside her. She clamped a hand over her mouth, but she could no more stop the laughter than she could stop hot lava from spilling out of a volcano. "I'm sorry…"

Bridget bent over in a fit of laughter, holding her side to keep it from hurting.

"I'm glad you're amused that my masculinity is suffering."

"Oh, darlin', it'd take a lot more than a cheap pair of sunglasses to hide your mascu—" She sobered, and the hand that hadn't been able to contain her laughter was once again clamped into place. Her mouth had gotten her into trouble again.

Sawyer turned toward her. The cheap lenses in his sunglasses failed to dim the smoldering look in his eyes. Bridget's eyes widened.

The trail wasn't as well traveled as the AT. In some sections, the overgrowth of weeds and briars hit midthigh on her, but there was a clear path. Up until this point, they'd been walking side by side, Sawyer on Bridget's right side, but now Bridget turned her back to the trail and faced Sawyer as he inched toward her.

"So my masculinity isn't easy to hide, huh?"

"Did I say that? I meant—"

"That I'm a manly man?" He wiggled his eyebrows, and she succumbed to a fit of giggles again.

The gap was closing, so Bridget quickened her pace.

Stepping into a hole, she lost her balance and tumbled backward. Sawyer reached for her, but the weight of her backpack pulled her out of his grasp. When she landed, there was a loud snap that sounded like a metal coil being sprung.

Sawyer's heart leaped to his throat, and his breath caught in a gasp.

Bridget's eyes widened. She struggled to get to her feet.

"Hang on." He reached for her flailing arms. "Be still. Let me help you. We don't know if there are other traps in the underbrush. I don't need you getting one of your arms or legs caught."

She stilled, and he knew his words had had the desired effect.

He quickly helped her to a seated position. Sure enough, there was an old, rusty jaw trap attached to the front of her backpack. He unfastened the sternum strap while Bridget sat as still as a stone statue. "Unfasten your waist strap," he barked.

She blinked, looked at him, then did as he commanded.

He slipped the pack off her shoulders,

hoisted it over her head and placed it on the ground in front of her.

Bridget paled.

The trap had attached to the rolled-up sleeping pad strapped to the top of the pack, right behind her head.

"That could have snapped my head in two."

He knelt beside her, willing his heart rate to return to normal. "Shh. Don't let your mind go there. You're safe. The trap didn't hurt you."

"Do you think *he* put it here?" Her voice quavered. "If I hadn't turned backward and tripped, you would have stepped on—"

He pulled her into his arms and stroked her hair. "Shh. It's okay. I've got you."

She shuddered, and a shiver raced through his body. From cold or from the embrace, he didn't know. But he refused to pull back. Even if he couldn't offer anything else, he could provide warmth to ward off shock.

"He's watching us, isn't he? Do you think he knew you were walking on that side of the path? Was he trying to take you out so he could get me?"

No use trying to sugarcoat his words. Bridget was too smart and would see straight through him. "I'd say the answer to all of those questions is most likely a resounding yes."

"Why not just shoot you?" Her face blanched. "I mean…"

"I know what you mean." He shrugged. "Lovelorn's actions over the past twenty-four hours have been erratic. Nothing like his normal MO. He's never used a gun before and his targets have always been females. You said the bullet would have hit you yesterday if Ryan hadn't stood when he did. Maybe Lovelorn isn't confident in his shooting ability after that incident."

Several moments later, Bridget sighed. "Well, then. We can't sit here all afternoon. As Grams would say, we need to stop burning daylight."

Sawyer reluctantly let her go. "You're right. But I want you to stay put while I see if I can get that trap off of your pack."

He stood and removed his backpack. Placing it on the ground, he searched for items that might be useful. A paracord. Nope. A Leatherman multi-tool. Aha. That might work.

He opened the knife and made quick work of cutting the straps off the top of the pack, releasing the pad with the trap still attached. Then he stood and searched for something to sweep the underbrush as they walked, to reveal any more hidden snares. Spotting a long, slender limb on a nearby tree, he closed the knife and flipped open the saw blade. The process was slow, almost like someone trying to use a nail file to cut a jail cell bar.

"What are you doing?"

"I'm trying to get this limb so we can use it to search for more traps."

"Sounds like a good idea to me." She wrapped her arms around her waist.

He instantly wanted to hug her again. Best to stop the direction his thoughts had taken. He sawed harder. The last fragment of wood snapped, and the limb was free. He cut off the end of the branch and removed all the leaves.

Satisfied, he flipped the blade closed and slipped the Leatherman into his pocket. Turning, he found Bridget dragging the trap and pad off the trail.

"What are you doing?" He rushed to help her.

"Moving it behind a boulder. We can pick it up after this is all over. I'm pretty sure these traps are illegal. If we find out Love-lorn didn't set it, we need to turn it over to the game warden. Don't you think?"

Once the trap had been safely deposited behind a rock, they gathered their gear and prepared to continue their journey.

Bridget slipped her pack onto her back, and her face contorted in pain.

"Are you hurt?" Sawyer couldn't believe he hadn't checked her for injuries.

She waved his concern away. "I'm fine. Just a little sore." She rubbed her shoulder. "And maybe a little bruised."

"Here, let me take that." He pulled the pack off her back before she could protest. Sawyer already had his pack strapped to his back, so he had no choice but to carry hers the way he would luggage. "You grab the limb I left leaning against the tree." He nodded to the walking stick he'd fashioned earlier. "I'll carry your pack, and you can be in charge of finding traps."

He bit the inside of his cheek to control the smile that wanted to escape at the sight of her wielding the small branch like a machete. She was taking this job seriously, and rightfully so.

Sawyer couldn't be sure, but he suspected a trapper, especially one using illegal snares, wouldn't have left their trap on a trail.

No. The trap had to be the work of Lovelorn. Sawyer had let his guard down a little with each mile they had covered on the trail, feeling like Lovelorn had a set game in mind and wouldn't attack until they had gathered all the clues. He wouldn't make that mistake again. Sawyer couldn't allow the killer to separate him and Bridget.

* * *

Sawyer shifted the pack to his other hand, and guilt flowed over Bridget. She wasn't pulling her weight. How could she be considered an equal if she didn't share the workload?

They reached an overgrown area, and she pressed the grass down with the limb—which was as long as she was tall—making a clear trail. The process was slowing down their progress, but she shuddered to think what could happen without this precaution in place.

"Are you getting tired?"

Bridget pressed a hand to her cheek. Tonight, when the sun went down and the temperatures dropped, she'd wish for warmth, especially without a pad to protect her from the cold ground. But for now, her face felt warm, most likely a combination of sun and windburn.

"I'm fine." Pain radiated from her neck and shoulder down her bicep, taunting her for not being completely honest.

A thud sounded. Sawyer had dropped her backpack onto the ground.

"Well, I'm ready for a break, and I think we're nearing the spot where the trail comes to a T. This may be the outcropping of rock in the last clue," he said, removing his pack.

"Come on, let's rest in the shade under these rocks while I check the GPS."

Bridget sat next to her pack on the ground beside Sawyer and moaned inwardly as her muscles cried in protest at the unyielding ground. She pulled her water reservoir out of her backpack.

"Maybe you can also locate a water source. We're getting low." She took a few sips, fighting the urge to drink it all. Best to conserve what she had.

A bulky, black two-way radio dropped onto her lap. "Here. I should have given you this already, but we've been kind of busy."

"A two-way radio? Do you plan on splitting up?" She heard the fear in her voice. Her throat constricted. *Please, Lord, let him say no. I'm not ready to be in the woods alone. Not yet. Maybe ever.*

"Of course not. However, if we get separated, I want you to have the ability to call for help."

She didn't tell him she had a tracking device on her finger; instead she held up the radio by the nubby antenna. "On this? Where we are, with all the mountains and valleys, a two-way radio won't have more than a half-a-mile range, tops."

A cocky grin appeared on his sun-bronzed

face. How did he look so good while she—
her hand pressed against her warm face, then
traveled up to her humidity-frizzed hair—
had to look like an overcooked lobster with
a bad perm?

"Contrary to what it looks like, that's not
a two-way radio." He pulled several things
out of his pack—food, socks, headlamp and a
plastic box with a first aid symbol embossed
on the top.

"If this isn't a two-way radio, what is it?"
she asked as he rummaged through the first
aid kit.

"It's a satellite phone. If you open the bat-
tery compartment, you'll see a latch that re-
leases the front cover so it'll slide down to
reveal the keypad."

Following his instructions, she quickly discovered the keypad and a small screen.

"If Lovelorn gets a look at it, he'll think the
same thing you did. He'd never believe that
we came out into the woods without some
kind of communication. But if he tried to use
it while it's in the radio position, all he'd get
is static."

"I remember you mentioned a satellite
phone earlier, but where did it come from?
It wasn't like you had time to plan for this
adventure."

"It was in my truck." There was that smile again. "I collect objects that look like one thing but in reality have an alternate purpose. I've always liked gadgets."

She opened her mouth to speak, but he rushed on. "I want you to carry it in your pack from this point forward. I've programmed Deputy Director Williams's number under speed dial. Call him immediately if there's an emergency. All you have to do is press this button here and then the number one."

A question burned on the tip of her tongue. She hated to question FBI protocol, but she had to know. "Is it normal for the deputy director to be so involved in the hands-on operations of a case?"

A pained expression flitted across Sawyer's face before he could mask it. He looked out across the ridge toward the mountains in the distance, and his eyes became vacant.

Bridget knew what he was seeing wasn't really there. "I'm sorry. You don't have to answer. I just never expected someone so high up in the Bureau to be an active part of an investigation."

"Vicki, the agent Lovelorn killed, was the deputy director's niece. I still don't know how Williams could forgive me for not protecting her. But he did."

Wow. She'd wondered why the deputy director had made a point of coming to the scene himself, but she hadn't expected this. Sensing Sawyer needed to say more and afraid the least distraction might interrupt him, Bridget bit back a comment.

"I owe him. He wouldn't let me wallow in self-pity. And tried his best to keep me from leaving the Bureau. The fact that he still believes in me, and my ability to bring this monster to justice—" His voice faltered, and he turned back to the phone still clutched in her hand. "This button activates the camera, and this one here…"

Sawyer pointed out several more features before leaving Bridget to examine the phone while he turned his attention back to the first aid kit.

"Aha." He held up a tube of ointment. "This should do." He opened the tube and squirted a white cream onto his finger, then started dabbing her face.

Bridget tried to pull back, but he grasped her chin and turned her toward him. "Hold still. This will only take a moment." He frowned as he rubbed the cream onto her nose. "I don't know why I didn't think to look and see what was inside the first aid kit sooner. I should have realized with your porcelain skin you'd burn easily, even in late November."

Through the years, her pale complexion had been called many things—sickly and pasty came to mind—but never porcelain. Porcelain sounded elegant and beautiful. Something she'd never been, and definitely something she didn't feel right now. Heat crept into her cheeks, and she prayed he couldn't tell she was blushing under her sunburn. She caught his hand and plucked the tube out of his fingers. "I can manage. But thank you."

He looked as if he wanted to argue, but didn't. Instead, Sawyer started putting things back into his pack. Once he'd completed his task, he started searching through her pack.

Bridget finished applying the cream to her face, replaced the lid and stowed the tube away in the first aid kit.

A few moments later, Sawyer emerged from the depths of her backpack with a victorious cheer. This time, he waved a white flag. No, not a flag. A hat. A floppy hat with a wide brim. "Seems Daniel thought of everything."

Sawyer turned the hat inside out, so the blue-and-green plaid lining was on the outside. He plopped it on her head and smiled like a little kid who'd scored the winning point in the big game. Her heart warmed, rivaled only by the heat radiating off her sunburned skin. No man—other than the men in her family—had ever taken care of her like this. She could get used to the attention.

Bridget needed to put distance between herself and Sawyer. Since she couldn't literally do so, she satisfied herself with twisting at the waist, stretching her sore muscles. Effectively breaking eye contact.

A sharp pain in her abdomen caused her to double over.

Sawyer was instantly by her side. "Are you okay? What's wrong? Where do you hurt?"

Bridget squeezed her eyes shut, willing the tears to stay at bay. She knew this pain well. It was from scar tissue. A lingering present from the man who'd stabbed her eleven times, causing her to lose her appendix, a kidney and her ability to conceive a child.

The pain was one more constant reminder of why she would never allow herself to fall in love. Even if she could have a child, who would want a woman with so many scars?

EIGHT

Sawyer watched Bridget do stretching exercises against a tree a few feet away. She'd insisted the pain in her side had simply been from overexerted muscles. He wasn't sure he believed her. First her shoulder pain and now this. Was it from the injuries she'd suffered from her accident? What had Frank said happened to her? An attack by an old boyfriend? A client she was protecting? Sawyer wished he'd paid better attention, but at the time, he'd been determined to keep things on a nonpersonal, need-to-know-only basis with his new bosses and coworkers.

He'd keep an eye on her. If it seemed her health was declining, he'd call for someone to extract her from the mission. He wouldn't put an injured or sick woman in a life-threatening situation. No matter how much he needed her.

He glanced in her direction once more before picking up the discarded satellite phone.

Time to check in. Sawyer flipped open the cover and accessed the control panel. He'd sent two messages earlier in the day, undetected by Bridget. Not that he didn't trust her to know what he was doing. Instead, he'd simply wanted to see how discreet he could be if the need should arise. One could never be too prepared.

There was a message from Hoyt. Check email. Sent picture of Jonathan. Ryan has been released. Doc said light duty until healed and then rehab. Take care of our girl.

Sawyer's reply was simple. Good news. Will guard her with my life.

He added their coordinates to the end of his message and hit Send. This way, the other agents would know where to start looking for them if they lost communication.

Sawyer pulled up his email and opened the image. His gut tightened. He hadn't expected to see his sister's face. The photo appeared to have been taken at a restaurant. Kayla and Jonathan leaned against each other, her face turned toward the camera and his turned slightly to the left looking at something off in the distance, obviously unaware the picture had been taken. A smile lit Kayla's face. She looked radiant.

Sawyer shifted his attention to the man beside her. He noted the arm draped across Kayla's shoulders and the hand resting over hers on the table. With short-cropped, dark brown hair, brown eyes and a square jaw, there was nothing unique about Jonathan's appearance. Wearing a dress shirt and tie, Jonathan appeared reserved—the complete opposite of Kayla's last boyfriend. Maybe his sister had picked a responsible mate.

He sighed. Time to get a move on. They'd been stopped too long. It would be dark in a few hours, and they needed to find the next clue and set up camp for the night.

Powering off the device, Sawyer slipped it into Bridget's pack. Man, he wished he'd been at the ranch when they'd received the command to go on the scavenger hunt. He could have brought several useful gadgets, like the tiny tracking device disguised as a safety pin or the camera disguised as a lighter. No point worrying about that now, but if he made it out of this alive, he'd do a better job of keeping his gadgets close.

"Sawyer! I found the turtle." Bridget's excited yell spurred him into action.

He scooted out from his resting place and found her pointing to a spot right above the outcrop of rocks where they'd taken shelter. "Look. About forty feet up. Someone painted that rock to look like a giant turtle's head sticking out of the mountain. The next clue has to be around here somewhere."

They raced to the base of the mountain and searched the ground, taking extra care to look inside small crevices between the rocks.

Then a thought hit Sawyer. He backed up, tilted his head, shaded his eyes with his hands and looked at the painted rock again.

"I know where the clue is." He pointed to the turtle. "It's up there."

Returning to his pack, he pulled the map out and spread it on the ground. "Remember, there was a short message—here." He tapped the drawing. *"I'm not aggressive, so don't worry about bites. You can find what you seek, if you're not afraid of heights."*

"The clue is in the turtle's mouth!" Bridget exclaimed.

"I thought the word *heights* referenced the spots where the trail narrowed and we were in danger of falling off the mountain." He assessed the situation as he spoke. The only way to retrieve the next clue was up. "Looks like I'm going rock climbing."

"You don't have a rope or harness. Or helmet."

He eyed the mountainside. "It'll be fine. There are several spots that look like good hand-and footholds. Not much different from many rocks I climbed as a child. Well, except it's about five times higher, but that's no biggie."

"Unless you fall."

He only half heard her as a sense of being watched came over him. The area was open, but there were still places for someone to hide. Sawyer swallowed.

Grasping Bridget's arm, he tugged her into a hug and whispered, "Stay still. Don't pull back. Lovelorn could be watching. I want you to get your backpack and go hide in the shelter of those trees. Go as deep as you can, but don't get too close to the edge of the mountain. After you're hidden from view, take the phone out of the pack. Turn it on and slip it into one of your pockets. You may need to find a way to stuff a couple of MREs in there, too, in case you have to ditch your pack—though only do that as a last resort." He pulled away from her, even though every fiber of his being cried in protest.

Green eyes mirrored the fear he felt. Fear of plunging to his death. Fear of Lovelorn killing one or both of them. Fear of being separated. Sawyer cupped Bridget's face and used his thumb to wipe the lone tear that escaped the pool in her eyes. His eyes never leaving hers, he lowered his head, stopping mere inches from her mouth. He whispered, "If you see Lovelorn, don't shoot unless you have a clear shot. Save your bullets."

He closed his eyes, and his lips claimed hers before he could talk himself out of it. When Bridget leaned in, as if wishing to prolong the moment, it took extra strength to resist the urge to extend the kiss.

Lord, I pray my impulsiveness didn't put a bigger target on Bridget's head.

"All right. I've got a mountain to climb." He forced his voice to return to a normal volume and tone and walked toward the rock overhang.

He waited until Bridget was hidden out of sight, then reached up with his left hand and found a crevice to grab hold of and started upward. And so it went. Inch by inch, he climbed until he reached a small ledge.

Sawyer stretched his right arm as far as he could and patted the ledge with the palm of his hand. He couldn't find anything to hold on to. He'd have to swing his leg onto the ledge, and then pull himself up. Pulling his arm back to the edge, he pressed his forearm against the rock with all his might.

He held tight and swung his leg up. And missed. Putting a little more swing and a lot more force behind the next attempt, he managed to get his foot onto the ledge, but then it slipped back down. Tiny gravel rained on him, and he ducked his head.

Come on, you can do this. Kayla and Bridget are depending on you.

Sucking in air, he held his breath and swung his leg for the third try. His foot caught, and with an added push, he rolled onto the ledge.

Air whooshed out of Bridget's lungs. She hadn't even been aware that she was holding her breath, but as Sawyer struggled to get onto the ledge, she realized how easy it would be for him to fall to his death. Or at the very least, end up with broken bones. Then what? They'd be sitting ducks for the serial killer who knew the path they were taking.

She'd almost forgotten. She'd asked the hostel owner for a pair of binoculars. Kneeling, she dug in her pack until she found them. This should help.

Bridget leaned against a tree and looked through the lenses. Where was he? She fiddled with the dials until she figured out the zoom and focus. Better. Much better. Sawyer appeared to be searching the forest, his gaze slowly moving from one side to the other before coming to rest on the area where she stood, hidden from sight. Could he see her?

He gave a thumbs-up. Guess that meant all was clear? They really needed to work on their secret communications. Like earlier, when she'd thought he was simply leaning in to keep from being overheard. If only she'd known he'd been about to kiss her, she could have... What? Pulled back? Prevented it? Or given in, and enjoyed the moment?

She sighed.

A soft thud sounded somewhere behind her, and the hair at the nape of her neck was brought to attention by the goose bumps popping out on her skin. Bridget pulled the binoculars away from her eyes and craned to look around the tree, careful not to make a sound.

She listened.

Silence. Not even the sounds of birds or other forest animals.

Had the noise come from somewhere else? They were out in the middle of the wilderness; maybe sound traveled great distances when it wasn't muffled by city noises. Looking through the binoculars again, she searched in the distance.

Nothing. All she could see were trees and mountains. A loud boom of thunder sounded. She jerked, searching the sky. There wasn't a single cloud.

The ground vibrated. An earthquake? In

Tennessee? Bridget spun back around to search the rocky mountainside and was greeted by a cloud of dust.

Not an earthquake. A rockslide.

Sawyer!

She swung the binoculars upward, desperately searching. She could barely make out the ledge through the dust. It looked to be intact, but there were rocks piled where Sawyer had been standing moments before.

His words came back to her. *I've programmed Deputy Director Williams's number under speed dial. Call him immediately if there's an emergency.* This had to be considered an emergency.

With one hand still holding the binoculars to her eyes, she reached with the other to pull the phone out of her back pocket. Wait a minute. Was that movement? She tilted her head and looked higher on the mountain. Yes. At the top. About ten feet above the painted rock, a denim-clad leg disappeared from view.

Sawyer was alive. She didn't know how he'd escaped the falling rocks, but he was alive.

She stooped and gathered her things. She pulled the MREs out of her pocket and shoved them back into the pack. Then she reached for the phone, but her finger froze midair above the power button.

What if it wasn't Sawyer? Had the killer been hiding, waiting for them, so he could cause the rockslide? Had the *boom* she'd thought was thunder been caused by the rockslide? Or had Lovelorn set off an explosion that caused the slide?

Bridget shoved the phone back into her pocket and reached for the gun in her ankle holster. She had to check on Sawyer, but she couldn't rush out there unprotected.

Lord, I know I've been self-absorbed for the past few months. And I've not had the best judgment lately. Please, guide my steps. Help me find Sawyer, and if he's injured, help me get him to safety.

If Lovelorn had caused the avalanche of rocks and was watching now, he would expect her to bust through the trees in the same general area she had entered them. She couldn't play into his hands. Leaving her backpack on the ground, she looped the binoculars over her neck and jogged toward a thicket of rhododendron about twenty yards to her right. The rhododendron extended beyond the tree line, stopping about ten feet from the base of the mountain.

There wasn't much in the way of cover beyond that point, but she had little choice if she wanted to get closer to the rocks to investigate. Ducking low behind the rhododendron, Bridget ran with all her might. As she reached the other side, a small boulder bounced down the mountain, missing her by mere inches, followed almost immediately by another.

She dived beneath the rock she and Sawyer had sat under earlier and covered her head to mute the sound of rocks raining down.

Dust swirled into the small space, causing her throat to tighten. She uncovered her ears and shifted into a seated position with her knees pulled up to her chest.

Realizing her mistake too late, Bridget yanked the neck of her T-shirt up over her nose. She concentrated on her breathing— willing herself not to hyperventilate. She was trapped.

Sawyer's muscles ached, but he couldn't stop now. Two more large rocks, then he'd be free. "Dear Lord, please let me get out of here. Don't let me die. I've got to protect Bridget."

He'd barely slipped back onto the ledge below the painted turtle after retrieving their newest clue when an explosion caused the rockslide, leaving him trapped beneath the rock that formed the turtle's head.

Now, he only needed to remove one last boulder, and he'd be free. Only this was the largest one. Sawyer put his back against the solid surface behind him, placed both feet on the boulder and pushed with all his strength. The rock didn't move. He'd have to climb over.

Getting down this mountainside safely was going to be harder than climbing up. Oh, how he wished he had rappelling equipment.

He puffed out his breath, placed his palms on the gigantic rock and heaved himself on top of it. Swinging his legs around, he sat with his feet dangling off the side and scanned the horizon. Where was Bridget? Had she stayed hidden like he'd prayed?

Sweat popped out along his brow. His heart raced. No, she wouldn't have stayed hidden. Not Bridget. She was fearless, or so it seemed. Always rushing headfirst into combat. Hadn't he seen that numerous times the last couple of days?

He needed to get off the side of the mountain. Patting the front pocket on his shirt, he verified the new clue was safely tucked away. Then he scooted to his right and found a foothold.

Five minutes later, he dropped to the ground. Weak from exertion. He wished he had time to sit and catch his breath, but that would have to wait until after he found Bridget.

The overhanging rock where he'd left his backpack was buried in rubble. He'd have to dig the pack out, but that, too, would have to wait.

Sawyer listened for sounds as he approached the tree line. Eerie silence greeted him. About fifteen feet into the forest, he stumbled—literally—over Bridget's backpack.

Hadn't he instructed her not to leave her pack behind unless it was an emergency? Hastening deeper into the forest, he whisper-shouted her name, over and over. He circled back to the spot where the backpack rested, praying he could find some clues.

From what he could tell, the only thing missing from the backpack was the satellite phone. Why hadn't she taken any of the MREs?

Maybe Lovelorn had caught her by surprise and taken her while Sawyer was being buried under rocks and rubble. Had the serial killer triggered the slide in order to get to Bridget?

Dear God, I thought I could protect Bridget on my own, but I can't. I realize that now. Sawyer dropped to his knees. *Lord, watch over that beautiful, impulsive woman. And, please, help me find her.*

A peace he hadn't felt in almost two years settled over him. It dawned on him that he'd prayed many times the past twenty-four hours without even realizing it. He had never made a conscious decision to turn from God. Rather, after Agent Miller's death, a feeling of unworthiness had caused him to stop attending church services, and soon the gulf separating him from the Lord grew even larger. How had Sawyer ever thought he could traverse the ups and downs of this life without the One who loved him most? *I'm sorry that I turned my back on You, Lord. Please forgive me. Show me the way to save Bridget.*

He needed to map out a plan. If Lovelorn had Bridget, Sawyer wouldn't do her any good unless he went in with a foolproof plan.

Snatching Bridget's pack off the ground, Sawyer marched back to the trail. He wanted to race after them. After all, they couldn't have more than a twenty-minute head start, but he couldn't be sure which way they'd headed.

He needed to look at the latest clue first. Maybe Sawyer could figure out where Lovelorn had taken Bridget.

Not willing to sit beneath the mountain of rock and risk another portion of it sliding down on his head, he stayed on the tree-lined side of the trail.

Sawyer dropped Bridget's pack on the ground beneath a maple tree located directly across from the turtle rock. He pulled the clue out of his pocket, forcing himself to take a few deep breaths to calm his racing heart.

The paper was another section of the map. He spared a glance at the mound of rock. If only the first clue wasn't buried under the rubble. He was sure the torn pieces would line up completely.

If only he'd had two satellite phones. He could contact Williams to see if Bridget's phone was transmitting. He could also text a picture of this clue to Hoyt. The other agents needed to know where he was headed next. And that Lovelorn most likely had Bridget.

He'd failed another woman.

Sawyer hoped Bridget had called Williams before being taken. He hated to admit he'd been wrong, but insisting on doing things his way may have been the biggest mistake of his life.

He followed the red line drawn on the map. The killer had circled a waterfall where the line ended.

This tranquil location hides a clue.
It's held up high with superglue.
Strength and agility you will need,
Or it will be impossible to succeed.
Be careful or you will get wet,
Because there isn't a safety net.

Ugh! He'd had it with this Shakespearean wannabe. Resisting the urge to crumple up the clue and burn the thing, Sawyer stuffed the paper back into his pocket.

He'd make one final sweep of the area. Though he knew if Bridget had been hiding somewhere, she would have seen him and showed herself by now. He took two steps and halted.

Was that someone talking? Standing as still as he could, he listened.

The faint sound of a voice reached his ears. Could it be the wind echoing through the trees?

He turned in the direction the sound came from. The rock overhang! He hastened to the rubble and leaned in to listen. Definitely a voice. And although he couldn't make out what was being said, he would recognize that chatter anywhere.

Bridget was trapped behind the rubble.

NINE

"Sawyer's probably injured. Or dead. And no one will ever find my body buried behind all these rocks. I can't believe I'm going to die like this." Bridget looked at the satellite phone. The pale yellow light from the screen cast an eerie glow into the darkness. She barely resisted the urge to throw the bulky gadget against the rock wall that held her prisoner. What good was the useless thing if she couldn't make a call when she was in danger? "Of course it won't work. There's no way to get a satellite signal inside this tomb.

"Why didn't I call Deputy Director Williams when I had—" She froze as her gaze fell on her ring. If only she hadn't refused to give in to Ryan's protective streak, she would've switched on the tracking device when she started on this journey. Too late now. If the satellite phone couldn't penetrate the rock wall that held her prisoner, neither would the tracking device in her ring. "I'm going to die. I don't know what's going to get me first, starvation or lack of oxygen."

She let out a frustrated scream. "I can't believe Lovelorn is getting away. And Sawyer—" Bridget's breath caught in her chest. She touched the tips of her fingers to her lips and tears pooled in her eyes. "Sawyer—"

"Yes?"

It couldn't be.

"Sawyer?" Bridget pressed against the mountainous wall and small gravel showered down beneath her weight.

"Bridget, are you okay?"

"You're alive! I thought you were dead. I thought Lovelorn killed you. I saw him—well, not him, but his leg. He set off an explosion to cause the rockslide. I didn't know what to do. I should have called Williams, but I didn't. I'm so sorry." The words tumbled out of Bridget like a freight train.

"Sweetheart. It's okay. I'm going to get you out of there. But it's going to take some time."

"What if I push from the inside? Do you think it'd give?"

"That's not a good idea. We can't risk the rocks caving in on you. Move back as far away as you can."

She pressed against the mountain and

bumped into something soft. Well, not soft, but softer than a rock. Turning, Bridget found Sawyer's backpack. She'd forgotten he'd left it here. Pushing the pack behind her back, she tried to get comfortable.

"Bridget, are you okay? Did you move away from the wall?"

"Yes. I'm as far away as I can get. Maybe two and a half feet."

"Good girl. Now sit tight, and I'll get you out of there." Muffled scraping sounds ensued, followed by an occasional grunt.

Time ticked by. Slowly.

A shadow moved. A spider? Her skin crawled as she twisted to get a better look. Thankfully, she'd fastened her headlamp to her belt loop that morning when the sun had risen. The small beam of light was the only thing keeping her sane at the moment.

Breathe. Inhale. Exhale.

"Sawyer... Sawyer!"

"Yes?"

Bridget broke out in a cold sweat, her heart racing. "It's not so much that I'm claustrophobic. I mean... I've never had problems in an elevator or anything. But the walls are closing in on me. It—it's like a tomb." She hated being weak. "Can we talk while you work? So I don't feel alone?"

He chuckled. "Sure. But I'm kind of busy trying to move these boulders, so you'll have to do most of the talking."

"Okay." Bridget prayed the wall between them filtered the anxiety out of her voice. "What do you want to talk about?"

Like fingernails on a chalkboard, the sound of rock scraping against rock caused a shiver to crawl up her spine and rattle her teeth.

"Um. I don't know. Your parents own a ranch in Colorado, right? Why don't you tell me what it was like growing up there."

"It was great. We had all the pets other children begged for, dogs and cats and horses. Of course, there was a lot of work involved, too. We had to take care of our own animals, as well as completing all our other chores."

"What chores did you have to do? Were there girl chores and boy chores?"

Images of her brothers came to mind. Nate wearing an apron, Ethan folding clothes, Ryan washing dishes, Charlie ironing and Hoyt vacuuming. "No. My parents didn't believe in dividing chores according to gender. Mom insisted her sons know how to cook and clean, while I had to learn to change a tire and check the oil and brake fluid." She smiled. "Mom and Dad didn't want any of their children to feel the need to get married ked. "Bridget!"

promised not to move, Cowboy." He
at the sound of her voice.

d you call me Cowboy?"

r head popped back through the narrow
ing, followed by her shoulders, which
shrugged. "I decided you needed a nick-
ne. Since you've worked on the ranch for
most a year, I think Cowboy fits. You got
problem with that?"

Her eyes gleamed. It wasn't so much of a
question as a challenge.

"I guess not." His muscles ached from
being held taut. "Are you about out?"

"Almost." She pulled his backpack through
the opening, and a rock jarred loose and
rolled down the pile, barely missing his head.
"Sorry."

"It's okay. But why didn't you leave the
backpack inside? I would have gone back and
gotten it after you were safe."

"What sense would that have made?"

He sighed. "Do you think you're secure
enough now that I can move and get on solid
ground?"

"Nope. But if you'll give me about five
seconds, I will be." She pushed the pack to
one side, sending more small rocks raining
down on him with a repeated "Sorry." Then

just to have someone to take care of them. We
were all raised to be independent."

Indistinguishable noises and grunts sounded.

"Are you okay?"

"Yeah." Sawyer groaned.

"Why don't I believe you?"

A rich laughter filtered into the space and
enveloped her in a hug, making her cheeks
warm almost as much as the kiss he'd given
her earlier had.

Bridget gave herself a mental shake. What
was she doing thinking of hugs and kisses?

"Girl, get a grip," she muttered as she
leaned her cheek against the cool rock wall
of the mountain. "You've fought too hard to
be taken seriously in a man's world. Don't
turn into a weak female now."

"What was that? Were you talking to me?"

Best to ignore his question and ask one
that was more pressing. "How much longer?"

"I think…ugh… I'm almost there." The
scraping sound seemed closer. "Okay, sweetheart, if I've calculated correctly, when I
move the next boulder, this wall is going to
tumble down—hopefully leaving an opening
that's large enough for you to climb through."

"Good, 'cause I'm ready to get out of here."

"I left my backpack under there earlier. Do
you see it?"

"Yes, I have it."

"Okay, I need you to sit with your back against the wall and pull your knees up to your chest. Then take my backpack and hold it in front of you. Kinda like a shield. Tuck your head behind the pack so no dust gets in your eyes. Okay?"

"Okay." She did as he'd instructed.

"Ready?"

"Ready."

She ducked her head, closed her eyes and prayed for God's protection.

Sawyer looked at the wall. He'd hoped to continue moving the debris piece by piece, but the structure was too unstable now that he had moved several of the smaller rocks and boulders out of the way. If his calculations were accurate, he'd have Bridget to safety in no time. But, what if his calculations were wrong? He shook those thoughts out of his head.

Climbing on top of the ledge and lying on his stomach, he tried to ignore the cold slab that sent a jolt through his body as he grasped the large rock that he planned to move. The sun dipped lower in the sky and shone directly into his eyes. Oh, what he would give to have those ugly, girlie sunglasses perched on his nose now. But he'd left them in his pack.

Lord, please let t

One. Two. Three. F and pushed with all h wall tumbled like a ho Dust mushroomed upwa his eyes. Covering his mou he waved away the dust cloud Blinking, he scurried to the sid grasped a sapling that grew out tainside and swung to the ground

The rock wall now lay in a heap, was approximately a two-foot gap the top of the rock pile and the ledge. was Bridget? Why hadn't she climbed the interior yet? Had too many rocks fa inside, trapping her even more?

"Bridget! Say something. Let me know you're okay." Sawyer clawed his way over several rocks. He had to reach the top of the mound.

Relief washed over him as her head popped through the opening. "I'm fine. But if you keep climbing and shifting the rocks like you are, I'm going to fall and break a leg or something."

Fear froze him. "I won't move a muscle."

An impish smile softened her dirt-streaked face, and Sawyer's gut tightened. Bridget appeared to struggle, and then she slipped out of sight.

He je

"You

stilled

"D

He

oper

she

nar

al

a

she grasped the ledge with both hands and pulled herself to a seated position on top of it. "Okay. I'm safe now."

Sawyer picked his way back to the ledge, hauled himself up beside her and pulled her into his arms. He laid his cheek on top of her head. "I'm glad to see you alive."

Her arms wrapped around his middle. "Me, too—I'm happy to see *you* alive, that is. I thought you died in the rockslide. But then I saw you. Only it wasn't you. And then—"

"Whoa. Wait a minute." He pulled back to look at her. "You thought you saw me after the rockslide?"

"Yes. But it had to be Lovelorn." She bristled. "I told you that when you first found me."

"I'm sorry. It must not have registered with me because I was focused on getting to you." He rubbed her shoulders. "Tell me exactly what you saw."

"I remembered I asked Daniel to pack me a pair of binoculars, so I was using them to watch you climb to the turtle—by the way, why did you give the thumbs-up sign? Could you see me? 'Cause I thought I'd done a good job hiding."

"No, I couldn't see you, but I knew where you were hiding. And I wanted to let you know everything was okay." The woman was exasperating. A person could get whiplash just listening to her talk. He raked his hand through his hair. "Bridget, sweetheart, can you please focus? Tell me everything you saw."

"I was watching you when I heard a sound behind me. I didn't know if the sound came from a person or an animal. Or a limb or something falling out of a tree. I turned to check it out, and then I heard a boom. At first I thought it was thunder but then the rockslide happened. When I turned back around, I couldn't see through all the dust. I was just about to call the deputy director, but the dirt settled, and I saw a leg disappear on top of the mountain. I thought it was you. When I went to investigate, rocks started falling again. I made the mistake of seeking cover under the overhang." She frowned. "I'm sorry. You should be farther down the trail looking for Kayla. My mistake slowed you down."

He offered her what he hoped was a comforting smile. They were behind, but it wasn't Bridget's fault. Lovelorn was playing games with them, that much was obvious.

Sawyer pushed to his feet, biting back a moan when his muscles cried in protest. "No apologies necessary. It was a natural instinct for you to dive under the overhang when the rocks started falling."

He wasn't about to tell her he suspected he had caused the second rockslide when he was disentangling himself from his own rocky tomb. "I'm just glad you aren't hurt. You aren't, are you?"

Bridget took the hand he offered.

"Only my pride. Nothing else." Her smile quivered, and somehow he didn't quite believe her.

He resisted the urge to question her further. "Let's get moving. I'd like to put as much distance as possible between us and this place before we stop for the night."

"Sounds good to me, but how do we get off this ledge without breaking a leg or something?"

"Follow my lead, and you'll be fine." Sawyer once again grabbed hold of the sapling, swung away from the ledge and dropped to the ground. Looking up, he glimpsed Bridget, with her arms wrapped around her waist, glancing toward the top of the mountain and then searching the tree line.

Was Lovelorn still out there watching them? Probably not. More than likely, he'd rushed ahead of them to set the next trap.

They'd been on the trail for almost twelve hours, and even though they probably had another forty-five minutes before darkness engulfed them, they had already placed their headlamps on their heads in anticipation.

Bridget couldn't remember a time when she had ever been more mentally and physically exhausted. Sawyer didn't seem a bit tired. Of course, he was most likely running on adrenaline and the desire to reach his sister as fast as he could. If it had been left up to her, they would have stopped and set up camp two hours ago, but she didn't have any right to complain. Not after costing them so much time with her carelessness.

A chill swept over her, and she rubbed her arms. The temperatures had fallen steadily all day and now hovered just above freezing.

"I promise, we're almost there. I know you're cold, tired and hungry." Sawyer walked beside her, quietly focused on finding the small cave Hoyt had mentioned in his last text. According to her brother, it would be the best place for them to set up camp for the night. They'd had to hike three-quarters of a mile off the trail, but the effort should thwart any plans the killer might have in the way of an attack and hopefully provide them with a somewhat restful night.

"I'm fine," she insisted even as the rumble of her stomach gave her away. Chuckling, she admitted, "Okay. I am cold, tired *and* hungry."

They walked on in silence, and Bridget contemplated how to bring up the questions she had about Sawyer's family.

Her mouth opened, and she snapped it closed. What right did she have to pry? Zero. Zip. None. She sighed.

"You might as well spit it out."

"What?"

"Whatever caused that heavy sigh."

"Couldn't it simply have been an *I'm tired* sigh?"

"Ah…no," he scoffed.

Stopping in her tracks, she asked, "Why not?"

Sawyer shrugged. "Your face gave you away. When you're deep in thought, you wrinkle your forehead and get a far-off expression in your eyes. Like you're trying to solve all of life's problems in a ridiculously tight time frame." He paused, then added softly, "Also, you mumble."

"I what?"

"Mumble. Under your breath. Kind of like you're arguing with yourself."

"I don't." While she denied it, she knew he spoke the truth. Even when she was thinking, she talked too much. "Okay, I might, occasionally, mumble."

A cocked eyebrow was his only response, the silence deafening.

"Fine." Bridget took a deep breath, stilling her nerves. "Yesterday, when I asked about your family, you said it was a discussion for another time. I just wondered if this was a good time."

A sad expression marred his handsome face. If she could've snatched the words back, she would've. *Lord, when am I going to learn to keep my mouth closed and mind my own business?*

"I wondered when we'd get around to this topic. I guess now is as good a time as any." He turned and started walking again. "You have to understand most of my information came from my mom. So, it's a little one-sided."

Bridget jogged and fell into step next to him.

"My parents grew up in a small town," he said quietly. "Mom was the daughter of the local school superintendent, and my father was the son of the town drunk. My mom, being younger and from a different social class, never hung out with my dad in high school.

"However, according to her, everyone knew my father's number one goal in life was to get out of that small town. Which he did by earning a basketball scholarship to Ole Miss. When Mom went to Ole Miss three years later, they ended up in a public speaking class together. Before the semester was over, they were dating. By the end of the school year, Mom was in love and planned to take him home to meet her parents. Sadly, my grandparents died in a tornado before Mom could tell them."

"Oh, how sad!" Bridget gasped, and covered her mouth with both hands. She'd meant to stay silent.

"Mom, an only child of only children, was an orphan. My father stayed by her side through the entire process. Going with her to plan the funeral and helping with legal stuff.

"My grandparents left a sizable life insurance policy to cover Mom's tuition and living expenses. Only Mom never returned to school. My father was accepted into NYU law school, and he convinced Mom to marry him and move to New York. She was nineteen."

"Oh, Sawyer—"

"She gave up everything for him," Sawyer continued. "Her dream of being an architect. And her inheritance. The plan was for her to put him through law school, and then once he got settled into a prestigious law

collect some water to treat with the tablets the hostel owner had packed for them. Bridget's throat was parched, and she was looking forward to a cool drink of water more than anything else. Well, maybe not more than she was looking forward to shrugging off the backpack. Her entire body ached.

"Here we are." Sawyer turned his headlamp on high beam and swept the light around the area.

There were a couple of trees next to the creek, and about a fourth of the way up the hillside, Bridget knew they'd find the small opening to the cave.

"Come on, let's go put everything in the cave. Then I'll come back down to the stream and collect water. Once treated, the water will have to sit for at least thirty minutes before we can drink it, so that needs to be one of the first things we accomplish." He headed up the embankment, but she stayed rooted to the spot. Sawyer turned back. "What are you waiting for?"

"Can't we sleep out here?" Her voice trembled, and she wrapped her arms around her body in a vain effort to control the shaking. "I've spent enough time in a closed-in space today."

She hoped she didn't sound like she was begging, though she really was.

He stepped toward her, but as he came closer, he faltered. She could sense that he wanted to argue with her, but he didn't. Instead, he went over to the two trees and strung a tarp between them. "I don't think it's supposed to rain tonight, but if it does, this will help. Of course, sleeping out in the open like this is going to be more dangerous, so one of us will need to be on watch at all times. I can take the first shift and wake you in a couple of hours."

Bridget would take her chances out in the open any day. At least then she'd stand a chance of seeing the danger that approached. She plastered a smile on her face and prayed, in the waning light, Sawyer wouldn't be able to tell how forced it was.

"Sleep's overrated." She joined him beside the trees, slipped her backpack off and grabbed the empty water container. "I'll collect water while you finish tying that off. Then we'll see what yummy meal is hiding inside those MREs."

Her touch of sarcasm had the desired effect, and his quiet laughter joined hers in a harmonious song as they went about setting up camp.

A short time later, their sleeping bags were rolled out under the tarp, and they were clearing the remains of their meal.

"That wasn't half bad, not at all what I expected. Except I'm sure my homemade lasagna would beat the so-called lasagna that was in your MRE any day. But my chicken, vegetables and noodles in sauce were quite tasty." Bridget focused on rolling her trash into a tiny ball to stuff in a corner of her pack.

"The lasagna wasn't bad. But then again, I was starving, so anything would have tasted like a gourmet meal. Of course, I'm sure the entire meal would have tasted much better heated." Sawyer caught her hand. "I'm sorry we can't build a fire. We can't take the chance of giving away our location."

"I understand." Bridget tugged her hand free and continued to gather their trash. "I'll tell you what the best part of the meal was. It was the Kreamsicle cookies. Yummy. They reminded me of childhood and eating orange sherbet on a hot summer's day. Oh, but don't let us forget the cold instant coffee. Now, that was a treat." Laughter died in her throat when she looked up to find Sawyer watching her.

Without a word, he drew her into a tight embrace. Why was he such a touchy-feely person all of a sudden? Did he think she was so fragile that she needed coddling? Perhaps he was using her as a sister substitute. Yeah, that had to be what he was doing. The strain of the day was probably crushing down on him, and he most likely wanted nothing more than to hug his sister close and protect her.

What about the kiss? Now that she thought about the events earlier in the day, she realized the kiss could have been a brotherly one. It had just been a peck, really. Nothing to worry about. Sawyer wasn't falling for her. When this was all over, they'd be able to go their separate ways without Bridget having to worry about protecting her heart.

She pulled away and busied herself, positioning her backpack behind her to be used as a cushion as she leaned against the tree. "I'll take first watch and wake you in a few hours. You need to get some sleep. You've worked much harder today than I have. After all, you had to remove two walls of rock."

"Are you sure?" He sounded both hopeful and offended. The thought of a woman protecting him while he slept was probably a blow to Sawyer's male pride.

Bridget smiled. "Yes, I'm sure. You need to be rested and alert tomorrow as we close in on this guy. It's the only way you'll be able to save Kayla."

"I guess I can't argue with that logic. I really am beat. Thanks, Bridget. Keep your gun handy and wake me if anything spooks you." He yawned and crawled into his sleeping bag. "I promise when we make it out of here alive—and we will—I'll take you out for a gourmet meal, complete with a dessert of your choice and a nice cup of hot coffee."

Unzipping her own sleeping bag and wrapping it around her shoulders, she sat with her back pressed against the tree and watched as snow clouds moved across the crescent moon. The sounds of coyotes and foxes yapping in the distance stirred memories of childhood and nights spent sitting on her grandparents' front porch. For a brief moment, she almost convinced herself to relax.

But then the moon rose higher in the sky and shadows danced in and out among the trees. Bridget hugged herself and whispered, "Stop. Do not let your fears take hold and change the reality. Sawyer is here. You have your gun. You are safe." *For the moment, anyway.*

She would not allow her thoughts to run away with her, making her relive her previous attack. Not now, when she was living an entirely new nightmare. At least this time she knew what was happening. A serial killer wanted to take her life. And if she planned to survive her second attack in a year, she couldn't let her focus falter.

TEN

Sawyer wasn't sure what awakened him. He lay perfectly still and listened. There. Was that a sniffle?

Like a child playing opossum, he opened his eyelids a fraction. He must have rolled onto his side in his sleep, because he now faced the tree where Bridget sat.

Barely able to make out her form, he was thankful for the small amount of light provided by the moon. She sat rigid with her sleeping bag wrapped around her like a blanket. As he watched, he noticed that she periodically touched her face. Was she crying?

What time was it? Even though he felt as if he'd just fallen asleep, he knew by the angle of the moon that the night was drifting away. He rolled onto his other side, sighed heavily, tried to mimic a snore and pushed his hands under his cheek. Discreetly, he pressed the button on his wristwatch, thankful that Mr.

Wingate, the building super who'd taken on the role of honorary grandfather when Sawyer was nine, had taught him the importance of being punctual and fostered a love for old-fashioned wristwatches.

Two thirty. He'd slept for five hours.

"You can stop pretending to be asleep. I saw the glow of your watch."

Uh-oh. Busted.

He stretched and then scooted to a seated position next to Bridget. Searching her face, he looked for signs that she'd been crying, but in the dark, it was hard to tell if her eyes were red and puffy.

"Why didn't you wake me?"

With a half shrug, she replied, "I figured you needed extra sleep worse than I did. After all, by my calculations, you haven't had more than a few hours of sleep since Saturday morning. Whereas I, on the other hand, grabbed a nap on Sunday while you hunted for information on Kayla's fiancé."

Why did he have a sneaking suspicion there was more to the story than she was letting on?

"You know it's not a competition to see who can go the longest without sleep, right?"

"I know."

"And we both walked the same distance yesterday—"

"Yes, but you did all that heavy lifting."

"You have to be just as tired as I am—was."

The way Bridget sat—like a stoic royal guard—looked uncomfortable.

"Turn and face that way." He pointed, indicating she should face away from him. When she looked like she was going to argue, he took her by the shoulders and turned her body so her back was toward him. Then he kneaded her taut shoulder muscles.

She twisted her head to look at him. "You don't have to—"

He planted a hand on top of her head and turned it back around. "Yes. I do. You're wound so tight there's no way you'll be able to relax enough to sleep. And I need you rested, so you can keep up tomorrow."

At least that was what he tried to convince himself was the reason for touching her. He couldn't allow himself to have feelings for her. Sawyer couldn't afford the distraction, not after letting so many women down already. Kayla. Agent Miller. And all the women Lovelorn had killed since he had taken over the case.

Bridget stopped her protest, and soon her head drooped. A few minutes later, he heard a soft snore. Smiling, he eased her to a more comfortable position with her head resting on her backpack. She was lying on top of her sleeping bag, so he unzipped his bag and pulled it over her. There. Once she was tucked in, he slid to the opposite tree. He needed to put space between them if he hoped to focus on the task at hand.

Keeping them both alive.

A few hours later, as the sun peeked above the mountains to their east, Sawyer prepared a cup of instant coffee for Bridget.

For the past hour, she'd been sleeping peacefully, but before that, she'd been restless and had talked in her sleep. He hadn't been able to make out what she was saying, just that she was frightened. He'd wanted to comfort her. But he'd been afraid if he woke her she wouldn't be able to go back to sleep. So instead, he'd stood guard with a feeling of helplessness deep in the pit of his stomach.

"Mmm…coffee." Bridget stretched and sat up. "I love the smell of—hey, you built a fire."

"Guilty as charged." He couldn't resist winking at her. She was so cute with her short hair sticking out in every direction and a crease on her cheek from using her backpack as a pillow.

"And it snowed." She untangled herself from the sleeping bag. "You must have been freezing. Why'd you put your sleeping bag over me?"

"I was fine. The tarp blocked most of the wind." He held out the cup. "Now come get your coffee."

"I thought you were afraid of alerting Lovelorn to our location."

"I'm hoping the smoke blends with the fog and isn't distinguishable from a distance. Plus, I figured it couldn't hurt too much at this point." He pointed to the trees they'd slept under. "I've packed the tarp and all our gear. We're ready to go as soon as you eat."

She accepted the cup he offered, pulling it under her nose and inhaling deeply before taking a sip. "Oh, that's so-o-o good."

"Glad you like it." He handed her a protein bar. "Now eat up. I've mapped out an exit route that will take us farther up the trail, eliminating unnecessary backtracking."

Bridget gulped her coffee before opening the protein bar. Then she stood, stuck the protein bar into her mouth to free up her hands, shrugged into her backpack and fastened the straps.

Sawyer watched, completely enthralled. Only three hours of sleep, and she was awake and ready to go without complaint.

She took another bite of the bar, smiled at

him and said, "Well, come on, Cowboy. We're burning daylight."

He didn't have to be told twice. He doused the flames, snatched up his pack and hurried to catch up with her.

"Are you sure we're going the right way?" Bridget asked for the third time in as many hours. She knew Sawyer probably thought she was being annoying, but she was convinced they'd passed that same maple tree twice already.

"Yes. I'm sure." He quickened his pace.

Bridget had to speed-walk to keep up. "Could we just take a quick look at the map? Please."

He stopped and turned so quickly she ran into him. "If we do, will it get you off my back?"

Yep. She'd obviously been a pest. She flashed a smile. "If I'm on your back, why do my feet hurt from all the walking?"

He groaned and shook his head, but even that couldn't stop a smile from spreading across his face.

"I know it was a silly joke. But I got you to smile."

"Fine, we'll look at the map one more time. It's probably time to stop and let you put on some sunscreen anyway. Before the sun gets higher in the sky." He located a spot in a shaded area.

Once they were seated, Sawyer took out the satellite phone and powered it on. Then he tossed the sunscreen to her. Finally, he pulled the map out of his pocket and spread it on the ground.

"Oh, I almost forgot." He started digging in his backpack again and emerged a few seconds later with the first clue. "I wanted to put the two clues together to see if it would give us additional insight."

While he lined up the torn pages just so, Bridget applied the sunscreen to her face. The lotion left a sticky residue on her skin that made her crave a long, hot shower. If she couldn't use the nongreasy, organic sunscreen that she had at home, she'd prefer not to use any at all, but she didn't have a choice unless she wanted to suffer from severe sunburn.

After she finished, she slipped the tube of sunscreen into the side pocket of her backpack. No point in Sawyer carrying the product when she was the only one using it.

Leaning forward, she tried to get a better look at the two maps side by side. "What do you think?"

He pointed to the spot where the maps

joined. "Do you see how our first clue fits under the other clue? It's twice as wide as the second clue. Kind of like he took the map, tore it in half horizontally, and then tore the top half in half vertically. Looks like we may only be missing one more section." He met her eyes. "If that's the case, this next clue will be the last one we get."

"And that clue is here? At the waterfall?" She pointed to the red circle on the map.

"Yes."

"Then I only have two questions. Where are we? And how much longer until we reach the next clue?"

She watched in silence as he picked up the satellite phone and started typing. He consulted the map, then typed some more.

"The best Hoyt and I can figure, we're about half a mile from the waterfall. But the terrain is overgrown and rocky, so it'll probably take us an hour to get there."

Bridget rooted around in her pack and found the jerky. "Fuel for our journey."

She tossed a pack to Sawyer, then tore open her own and stuck the hickory-smoked, leathery treat in her mouth. Biting down, she slipped her backpack on and fastened the straps.

Once the pack was securely in place, she

grasped the jerky, bit off a piece and began to chew. She was acutely aware of Sawyer watching her the entire time.

Had he guessed, the jerky—like the protein bar earlier—provided her something to bite down on to keep from crying out in pain as she put the heavy backpack on her shoulders?

Sawyer wasn't buying Bridget's act. He knew the past two days had been as grueling on her as they'd been on him. She was in pain. That much was obvious. Agony flashed in her eyes every time she put on her backpack.

He wished she'd talk to him and tell him the cause of the pain and what he could do to help. But he knew that wouldn't happen. She was one of the most stubborn women he'd ever met, determined to prove her independence no matter how much pain she had to endure. He couldn't help but wonder if her need to prove herself and her independence had anything to do with five overprotective, doting brothers.

Of course, he didn't blame Bridget's brothers for being protective. If Sawyer could've been a part of Kayla's life while she was growing up, he was sure he'd have treated her the same way. And then maybe, just maybe, she wouldn't be in the hands of a killer right now.

Instead, he and Kayla were practically strangers. Adult siblings trying to forge a relationship that should have been cemented years earlier, who had bimonthly phone calls filled with awkward silence.

He planned to change that if he—no, when he—rescued her. Two phone calls per week at a minimum and weekend trips to visit each other at least once every two or three months would be the first thing to change. He wanted to know his sister. And her fiancé.

Her fiancé won't be as easy to discover, since I left him hidden under cover.

"We forgot Jonathan."

"What?" Bridget asked.

"When we worked our way back to Lovelorn's trail this morning, we approached it at an angle, missing a section about two miles long." He stopped and pulled his satellite phone out of his pocket. No time to waste texting. He'd have to pray that Lovelorn wasn't close enough to see or hear him making a call.

Agent Anderson answered on the first ring. "Eldridge, is everything okay?"

"Anderson, I know we discussed not sending any agents in until Bridget and I reached the last clue, but I'm afraid we may have skipped the section of trail where Jonathan has been hidden." He shoved his free hand through his hair. "I don't know if he's alive or not. If he is, I'm sure he'll need medical attention. ASAP. I need agents on the trail immediately."

"What about Lovelorn? I thought you were afraid he'd kill another innocent bystander if we didn't play by his rules."

"I'm pretty sure he's keeping a close eye on us, so I don't think he'll see the team if they are that far behind us."

"What makes you say that?"

"Bridget saw him yesterday at the turtle rock."

"She saw him? What'd he look like? And why are you just now reporting this?"

"There wasn't anything to report. She didn't see his face. She only saw his leg as he disappeared on top of the mountain after the explosion that sent the rock pile down on me. It's most likely he's waiting for us at the next clue. Which means—"

"He won't see the agents."

"Not as long as they stay far enough back. So make sure you don't send any overeager rookies out here, okay? The last thing we need is for someone to rush in and try to be a hero."

"Look, Eldridge, I know you have a lot at stake here, but I know how to do my job. You just worry about keeping yourself and those two ladies alive. Okay?"

"Yes, sir."

"And just so you know. Agent Vincent, along with another agent and a medic, are already on the trail. Have been since noon yesterday. They got on the trail at a different starting point, and have been maintaining a slow-and-steady pace to not send up any alarm signals if Lovelorn saw them. I'll alert them to pick up their pace, but they are still several hours behind you." With that, Anderson disconnected the call.

Bridget placed a hand on his arm. "Sawyer?"

"Huh?" He didn't understand the puzzled expression on her face.

"I asked you if they were going to send agents to look for Jonathan."

"Oh. Yes."

She raised an eyebrow. "Then why do you look so concerned?"

Sawyer shook his head. "It's nothing. Probably just the lack of sleep."

"Most likely." She smiled. "Even though Agent Anderson and Hoyt aren't out here on the trail, I'm sure they're not getting a full night's sleep, either."

Exhaling a breath, Sawyer smiled. "You're probably right, but Hoyt is on the trail. Apparently, he and another agent are a few hours behind us. Now let's get a move on. That waterfall should be just around the next bend."

The next bend ended up being fifteen minutes and two-tenths of a mile away.

Sawyer heard the rush of the water as soon as they rounded the curve in the trail. He immediately began searching, looking for hiding spots for Lovelorn, but there didn't appear to be any. This area didn't have the amount of clustered trees or thick foliage they had seen along the rest of the trail.

And this made him nervous. Not because there were no places for the serial killer to hide, but because there were no places for Sawyer to hide Bridget if the need arose.

ELEVEN

The scenery was breathtaking. Everywhere Bridget looked, she saw God's beauty—trees and rocks covered with a dusting of snow, the peaceful flow of the waterfall carved into the mountainside, icicles around the edges of the water.

The waterfall had a vertical drop of about thirty-five feet and fell into a plunge pool that emptied into a stream. The water sparkled as the stream wound through a moss-covered, rocky forest full of trees and a scattering of ivy.

The pool would be an inviting place to swim in the summer. Honestly, if the temps were twenty degrees warmer, she would be tempted to dive in and rinse the trail dirt off of her aching, clammy body. But the last thing she needed was hypothermia. She sighed.

"That was a heavy sigh."

She'd been so wrapped up in the scenery

that she'd almost forgotten Sawyer stood in close proximity. Almost, but not completely. Always alert and protective, his stature and demeanor, albeit guarded, commanded attention.

Exhaustion dragged at her limbs; she didn't know if she could go on. What was the point? After all, no matter how she looked at it, there was an enormous chance Lovelorn was going to murder her. So why keep playing his ridiculous game?

"It's nothing. I'm just saddened that a serial killer has tainted this beautiful place. I would love to be able to take time and enjoy listening to the waterfall as I sat over there on that rock ledge and read my daily devotional. Instead, I'm looking for a clue that's going to lead me closer to a trap." Bridget knew she was complaining but couldn't seem to stop herself. She'd tried to stay positive, but she was tired and sweaty and in pain. "I don't know why I refused to let Ryan take me to a safe house. I would have been in a warm location with a soft bed and plenty of junk food in the fridge. If Lovelorn tracked me down and killed me, at least my last days would have been comfortable, not like—"

When was she ever going to learn to control her tongue? She'd been doing so much better about it until now. Heat crept up Bridget's neck and flooded her face, which she knew from experience meant her face was an ugly, splotchy red.

For the longest time, Sawyer didn't say a word. He just stood there, rubbing his stubble-covered chin, his brow furrowed.

He reached for his backpack, which rested on the ground next to hers. "I'll call Hoyt. Tell him it's time to send in a team to extract you. I'll go the rest of the way alone."

Placing her hand on his arm, she halted his actions. "That won't be necessary. I'm not about to let you walk into a trap alone. And in all honesty, I am always restless when I'm the bodyguard at a safe house. There's no way I could ever be the person in protective custody. It would be pure torture." She lifted her eyes toward Sawyer, intending to apologize for being whiny, but movement in her peripheral vision caused her to gasp. "I know where the clue is."

Without giving him a chance to respond, she raced up the mountain toward the top of the waterfall. Thankful she had removed her pack when they first arrived, Bridget zig-zagged around rocks and jumped over logs, ignoring Sawyer's calls for her to stop.

The only reason she reached the crest before him was because she had taken off without giving him warning. A sudden cramp caused Bridget to double over, holding her side in pain.

When Sawyer reached her, he grasped her arm and pulled her around to face him. "Never do that again. What if Lovelorn is watching us? He could've shot you."

She took a deep breath and slowly released it. "He could've. But I think he's enjoying watching us play his game. Now, do you want to know where the clue is or not?"

"You can be infuriating, did you know that?" He raked his hand through his hair. "Of course I want to know where the clue is."

A snicker threatened to escape, but she tamped it down. Sawyer probably wouldn't understand giddiness brought on by sleep deprivation.

"The killer's clue said *it's held up high with superglue* and *be careful or you will get wet*." She smiled, grasped his arm and turned him to face the waterfall. "See that oak tree? Look at the limb that's hanging way out over the falls. It's hard to tell exactly what it is from here, but it looks like—"

"A piece of paper inside a plastic storage bag." He turned back toward her, one eyebrow raised. "How did you see that from where we were?"

"I saw something flap in the breeze. When the sun hit it, I realized it was too shiny to be a leaf, so…" She turned her hands out, palms upward, and shrugged.

"Okay, guess I'm going climbing again."

She trailed behind him as he went to examine the tree. Once they got close, the enormity of the task became obvious. The lowest limb was higher than Sawyer could reach. He bent at his knees, obviously preparing to jump to reach the limb.

Bridget placed a hand on his shoulder. "Why don't you let me climb the tree?"

"No. Absolutely not." He shook his head vigorously. "Every clue has either been a trap or led to one."

"Exactly my point. All of Lovelorn's traps have seemed to be aimed at you. The tree looks solid, but the limb the clue is on isn't very big. Your weight is likely to break it, sending you tumbling to your death. Whereas…" She stepped back with a look-at-me pose. "I'm at least sixty pounds lighter than you. Meaning I'm the only one with a chance of snagging the clue without breaking the limb."

He bent and looked her in the eyes. "If I can't reach the first limb, how do you plan to?"

"I'll get on your shoulders, and you can lift me up."

"No. Absolutely not. I can't let you do that. I promised your brothers I'd keep you safe." He turned to head down the mountain. "I'll go get the paracord out of my backpack. I should be able to use it to rig up a climbing saddle of some sort. I can climb to the bigger limb that's higher up and use the paracord to lower myself down to get the clue."

She put her hands on her hips. "And how much time will you have wasted if it doesn't work?"

Sawyer stopped in his tracks and turned back to her. She squared her shoulders and met his gaze. "I'm actually a pretty good climber. Why not let me try? If I can't reach the limb or if I see something that makes me think it's unsafe to continue, I'll come down. Then you can do it your way, and I won't say another word."

"Are you sure you can manage? Your muscles have to be sore after two days of hiking. And your shoulder's been hurting. You could slip."

Obviously, she hadn't hidden her discomfort very well. "If I can't get a good grip, I won't take a chance. I promise."

"Okay. It's not like we have much choice."

He took her hand and led her to a nearby boulder, and helped her on top of it. Then he knelt in front of her. Bridget put her hand on the top of his head to steady herself and draped one leg, then the other, over his shoulders.

"Hang on tight." He placed one hand on her left leg and used the other to push himself upward.

Holding her breath, Bridget tried to quell her nerves. *I can do this. It's my chance to show that I'm not helpless. Please, Lord, let me be successful.*

"Can you reach the limb?"

"Almost." She stretched with all her might, but fell short by a couple of inches. "I need to stand on your shoulders."

"Absolutely not." He tried to walk away, but she grabbed hold of the tree and clung to it.

"It's our only chance."

"Fine." He stood perfectly still as she eased herself into a standing position, his hands clamped on her feet.

"I got it! Let go of my feet. I'm going to swing my leg over the limb."

In a matter of minutes, Bridget was straddling the branch that held the clue. She leaned forward, almost completely lying down on top of the limb. Employing an inchworm-type movement, she slowly worked her way toward the end, where the letter was attached.

"Slow down. Take your time. That's it… go easy."

Knowing his control issues, she tried not to let Sawyer's commands distract her.

"You're almost there, just another two feet. You're doing great."

"Sawyer." Despite the cold temps, sweat rolled into her eyes, making them sting. She blinked to clear her vision. "I know you're trying to be helpful, but you're making me nervous."

Bridget glanced down to give him a reassuring smile and nausea swept over her as she glimpsed the water swirling below. Pressing her lips together, she quickly shifted her gaze to Sawyer.

He gave a thumbs-up and remained silent.

She inched forward, sliding her hand along the bark to maintain contact. Stretching her arm out, she tried to reach the plastic bag. Almost. She would have to go farther to the edge.

As she slid along the next section of the branch, the bark peeled. *Hmm. That's strange.* "Sawyer? Something doesn't feel right."

"What do you mean? What's wrong?" She could hear the urgency in his voice.

Bridget slipped a fingernail under the next section of bark and it peeled off, falling into the water below. Her heart raced. She tried to keep her voice neutral. "There are saw marks."

"What?"

"It looks like he tried to hide them, but as I moved across this section, the bark peeled."

"Get down from there. Now!"

Her hands were covered with scrapes and cuts and her shoulder burned, but she wasn't about to give up. The clue was less than six inches outside her reach. "I'm too close to give up now. Besides, I think I can get the clue and get down safely. Given my size, I'm sure Lovelorn wouldn't expect me to climb the tree. It doesn't look like the saw marks go that deep. I'm sure I'm light enough to do this."

"Bridget Vincent." Stretching each syllable of her name, he sounded so much like her father that she would have laughed if the situation weren't so serious. "Don't make me come up there and get you."

"That'd make sense, wouldn't it? Let's add extra weight to the limb and see if it'll hold up. Besides, if you could've reached the first limb, I wouldn't be up here, would I?" She had to crane her neck to look backward far enough to see him. "It'll be okay. I promise."

Easing forward and leaning low, she closed

her fingers around the bag and yanked. It didn't budge.

One more time. She pulled with all her strength. The limb made a cracking sound. She had to hurry.

Sparing another look in Sawyer's direction, she noted the grim expression on his face as he stood quietly, watching her every move. *Lord, whatever happens, please let me get the clue so Sawyer can save Kayla.*

If she inched forward another two inches, right up to the edge of the saw marks, maybe she could open the bag and pull the paper out. Biting her lower lip, she pulled her knees forward, pressed tightly against the tree and extended her upper body, with her arm outstretched.

A reverberating splintering sound echoed in the silence. And she hurled through the air.

"No-o-o…" The protest ripped from Sawyer's chest as Bridget plunged into the waterfall. Instinctively, he wanted to dive in after her, but common sense took over. And he raced down the side of the mountain.

As he neared the plunge pool, he saw her come up out of the water a few feet from the recirculating current at the base of the falls. Relief was short-lived when she disappeared out of sight again. Sawyer pulled off his shoes, jerked the holster and gun free from his belt and dropped them onto the bank. He ran into the water, sucking in his breath through clinched teeth as the icy cold liquid lashed at his body, and swam toward her. Slowed by the weight of his saturated clothes, he watched in agony as she surfaced, gasped for air and disappeared again.

As he neared Bridget, he could feel the change in the circulation of the water below him. If he got too close to her, they'd both be pulled under.

When she broke through the surface for the third time, he was ready with his arm outstretched. He clasped her wrist in a vise grip and pulled. *Come on.* One more tug, and she was free of the swirling waters. Flipping her onto her back, he put one arm around her chest and used the other to swim them to shore, each stroke taking more effort than the previous one. Either his muscles were more fatigued than he thought, or Bridget weighed much more than she looked. Or both.

He pulled her onto the bank. That's when he saw the end of the branch—the clue still intact—clutched in her hand. No wonder she'd felt so heavy. That hunk of wood had to weigh at least forty pounds.

Bridget coughed, and he rolled her onto her side. Water streamed out of her mouth. Sawyer lifted her head off the rocky bank and supported it as she continued to cough and purge the water.

"What were you thinking? That tree limb almost caused you to drown."

Her eyelids fluttered opened, and emerald eyes melted his heart.

"But it didn't," she whispered, her breath coming out in a puff of fog. "I saved the clue. And you saved me."

"This time. But you can't—" He was gearing up to lecture her but faltered when she struggled to sit. The neck of her flannel shirt slipped off her shoulder, revealing three jagged red scars. Scars that he recognized as knife wounds. The smallest scar was precariously close to the jugular. The second one was under the collarbone, and the longest of the three started at the deltoid and ran down the bicep.

Sawyer wasn't aware he was gaping until Bridget snapped, "Close your mouth." She tugged the wet shirt back into place. "I would've thought you'd seen scars before."

"Of course I have." He swallowed. "I knew you'd been injured. I just didn't expect to see knife wounds. Those are knife wounds, aren't they?"

Drops of water dripped down her face, and Sawyer wondered if a few might be tears. An icy wind swept over him, chilling him to his bones and bringing him back to the most pressing matter at hand.

"We need to get dry before we freeze to death. Then you can tell me about your scars." He stood and extended a hand to help her up. "Grab your backpack and go behind that boulder and change your clothes while I build a fire."

"What about…the…smoke? Won't…it alert… Lovelorn…we're here?" Bridget asked between chattering teeth.

"I don't see that we have much choice. Ice crystals have formed on your eyelashes." He touched her face, his eyes drawn to her mouth. "And your lips are turning blue. Now, go. The sooner we get dry, the sooner we can get out of here."

Sawyer scanned the area. Where was he going to find dry tinder to start a fire? Most of the woods were still covered in a light dusting of snow, and the few areas where the sun had melted the snow were too wet.

He searched along the mountain under an outcropping of rocks. Next, he rummaged under low-hanging evergreen bushes. Before long, he had gathered a satisfactory number of small limbs and twigs. Digging through his backpack, he collected the wrappers from their meals. Then, he used one of the larger sticks to clear a section of the ground, sweeping away the snow and digging down to dry dirt.

Bridget reappeared, wearing dry clothes and a Mylar solar blanket wrapped tightly round her. Sawyer had forgotten about the blankets Daniel had put into their backpacks. He really owed the hostel owner for sending them on the trail with the tools they needed to survive a situation like this.

Concentrating on building the fire, Sawyer remained silent and waited, hoping Bridget would tell him about the scars but knowing he couldn't push her.

Several minutes passed, then she spoke in a whisper-soft voice. "It was a fluke, really. One of those weird coincidences that no one can explain. I had run that trail almost daily for four years. And I'd seen him—spoken to him—for three years. We were on a first-name basis. Exchanged pleasantries. His name was Robert."

"How many times did—" He'd never been at a loss for words. Today, he was. *Way to go, Sawyer. Now she'll think her scars repulse you, and she'll be self-conscious.*

"Eleven. The three you saw. One on my right hand where I tried to defend myself. Two on my left arm. One in the back, barely missing my spinal cord. And four in the abdomen." She trembled, and he suspected it wasn't only from her recent icy plunge.

The fire was roaring now, and she came closer, warming her hands over the flame. Sawyer wanted to pull her into his arms and comfort her, but he'd already blurred the lines too many times. He knew his overprotective instincts sometimes came across as flirtatious, and he couldn't let Bridget think his interest was more than friendship. Though he knew she wasn't interested in him, she was vulnerable, and that was enough reason to keep his distance.

"Why did he attack you?"

"As far as Robert knew, I worked for an insurance company." The green eyes that had shone so brightly earlier now had a darkness to them that shook him to his core. "Not really a lie since a bodyguard is a type of insurance."

There was no reason to explain her cover to him. He understood better than most people the importance of separating work from one's personal life, but he suspected she needed to let it out.

"What I didn't know was that Robert was really Dr. Robert Covington the third."

"The heart doctor that was married to that country music star? When she left him and filed for divorce, he couldn't handle it and—"

"Stabbed one of her bodyguards. Yes. The man I'd exchanged pleasantries with for years suddenly wanted me dead because some paparazzi took a picture of me guarding his estranged wife." A chuckle escaped her lips. "You want to know something funny? I wasn't even supposed to be the bodyguard that night. The person who was supposed to protect her had the flu."

"He stabbed you just because you were in a picture with his estranged wife?"

"No. He stabbed me because I wouldn't tell him where she was hiding. As the date of the divorce hearing drew closer, he started harassing her, becoming increasingly more threatening. It had been decided, after that one last public event, she'd take a vacation at an undisclosed location and not return to the States until the day before the hearing." Bridget let out a soft sigh, the only indication of the difficulty she was having retelling the story. "He attacked me an hour before her plane landed on US soil."

They sat in silence. There was nothing

left for her to tell. The news had been full of the story and the manhunt that ensued. Sawyer knew that Robert Covington was apprehended a few hours after the attack and now sat in prison awaiting his attempted murder trial. As the victim, Bridget's name had been kept out of the news as she underwent surgeries and rehab. Though he highly doubted she could stay anonymous once the trial started and she had to testify.

The fact that he had not put two and two together and realized she was the one Robert Covington had attacked was further proof of the lengths he'd gone to, to distance himself from his life in law enforcement. He had no words.

Unable to resist the urge to hold her, Sawyer wrapped his arms around her and pulled her to his chest. He ran his fingers through her hair, brushing it away from her face.

She stiffened and his hand stilled. Pulling back, she looked him in the eyes and without wavering said, "The deepest scars aren't seen."

As a psychologist and having dealt with his own turmoil the past eighteen months, he knew the truth in her words. "I know—"

"Yes, I'm sure you do. But what you don't know is what it's like to wake up in a hospital bed and have the doctors tell you 'Congratulations, you'll live but there's irreparable damage.' Then a few days later have your boyfriend tell you 'No man will ever want to marry you now.'"

He gasped for air. It wouldn't have been any harder to breathe if she would have punched him in the solar plexus. How could any man say those words to her? No matter the damage. And he could only imagine how extensive it had been given she'd been stabbed so many times. He ached to comfort her but feared he'd be rejected again.

Bridget flicked her head toward the limb that lay at the water's edge, the note still attached. "Now that you know my life history, why don't we focus on what brought us here. Let's figure out how to catch the creep who's determined to kill us."

TWELVE

Sawyer's mind reeled with all the information that had been jammed into his brain since that first shot rang out nearly sixty-eight hours earlier. Bridget's willingness to put her life on the line so soon after almost losing it humbled him.

He was a selfish moron for having dragged her into the wilderness. If only he'd taken time to think things through, he could have come up with a better solution. Instead, he'd allowed Lovelorn to have the upper hand.

"Are you almost finished?" Bridget's voice sounded from the other side of the boulder. "I've been looking at the clue, but I can't make heads or tails of the map."

He fastened the last button and stepped into view. "I have an idea what it means, but I'd like to put some distance between us and this place before we discuss things." Plucking the clue out of her fingers, he read the cryptic message once more.

You succeeded in getting the final clue,
But I promise, I'm still smarter than you.
While the journey has been fun,
There's no erasing what must be done.
If you find the cabin where Kayla awaits,
Be prepared to bust open the pearly
gates.

"I scanned the area while you changed. Didn't see a thing. I don't think Lovelorn is hiding anywhere watching us. But we can't rule out that possibility. We're at his mercy when we're at a location of his choosing." Sawyer stuffed the clue into his shirt pocket. "There are several trails in and out of this location—too many for him to control. Our only hope is that he's gone on ahead to wait for us and doesn't see which trail we take, allowing us time to plan our attack."

The backpacks lay on the ground at their feet. He knelt beside them and pulled the binoculars out of Bridget's pack. "Here. Scan the area while I organize our stuff. By my calculations, taking the shortest route would put us about five hours from our final destination, which puts us six and a half hours ahead of schedule." Sawyer moved everything he could to his pack, leaving Bridget with the bare minimum—sleeping bag, two MREs, water, chlorine tables, the satellite phone, matches and her headlamp.

"And if we take the longest route?" Bridget questioned.

"We'll be too late." Sawyer stood and shrugged into his backpack. "Did you see anything?"

Bridget shook her head. "No. Nothing."

"Good." He took the binoculars from her and slipped the strap over his head. "All right, let's go." He picked up her pack and headed northwest, away from the falls. "I figured we'd make our own route. Lovelorn wouldn't—"

Where was Bridget? Looking over his shoulder, he saw her rooted to the spot where he'd left her. "What are you doing?"

"I could ask you the same thing?"

"What do you mean?"

She glared at him, her hands on her hips. "Why are you carrying my backpack? I'm no more helpless now than I was before you saw my scars."

"I know that."

"Do you? Really? Then why'd you put half the stuff from my pack into yours?" He opened his mouth to protest, but she barreled on. "Don't deny it. Just because you tried to divert my attention doesn't mean I'm clueless. Most of the time, I'm very alert. Just because Robert was able to—" Her voice cracked, and she looked down at her feet. "Doesn't mean I'm not capable of taking care of myself. Or of doing my share."

How could he have been so insensitive? He'd seen the scars and treated her like an invalid. No wonder she was mad. Sawyer closed the gap between them and held the bag out for her to slip into. "You're right. I shouldn't assume that you need or want help. You've done just fine carrying your own weight. I'm sorry." He turned her to face him, adjusted straps and fastened clasps. "My only excuse is I'm protective by nature. I didn't mean to insult you."

Bridget touched his cheek with her ice-cold hand and a smile more beautiful than any he'd ever witnessed shone on her face. "Thank you."

He caught both her hands in his and attempted to warm them.

Pulling back, she broke contact. "What about the stuff you took out of my pack? Wouldn't you rather redistribute it?"

"Nope." With that, he turned and headed

back toward the trail. She'd better follow, or he'd leave her here. Alone in the forest. No. He wouldn't.

Stubborn woman. He had let her have her backpack, but there was no way he would add more weight to the pack.

Keep walking. Don't look back.

He had to tread lightly. She'd bared her soul and shown him raw emotion earlier. The urge to coddle her was strong, but he knew doing so would be a big mistake. It was obvious her ex-boyfriend was a major jerk who took great pride in making her feel like less of a woman.

Bridget telling him about the man's words when she had—while he was trying to offer comfort—was her way of putting up walls. And Sawyer had to do what he could to keep her from erecting them too high.

The sound of a footfall landed beside him. "When I looked at the map, there seemed to be five different ways to leave the area of the waterfall. What made you choose this one?"

"Process of elimination. Lovelorn would expect us to take the shortest route, so that's not a wise choice. We also can't take the longest route, because it would put us past our deadline getting to Kayla."

"And you're still convinced that midnight

on the twenty-third is tonight, not tomorrow night?"

"Yes. Absolutely."

"Okay, so that leaves three routes."

"I've marked them from the shortest to the longest. But we have no way of knowing which trails Lovelorn rigged with a trap."

"So…"

"We take the longest of the three. The one he will least expect, because it will put us getting to Kayla at the last possible minute."

"What? Why would you choose that route?"

"When I looked at the map, I noticed a stream that crosses all the routes at various points, going at a diagonal."

"I saw that, too, but the area looked like a densely populated forest. Won't that make navigation more difficult?"

"There's been less rainfall than usual the past few months. Not enough to put the area in a drought, but hopefully the water will be low enough for us to walk along the edge of the stream and not be in the overgrown areas." Sawyer's chest tightened, and he puffed out a breath. "Following the stream allows us to move between the paths, avoiding traps. Giving us our only hope of reaching Kayla in time."

Sawyer prayed he'd chosen wisely.

* * *

Bridget trailed along behind Sawyer, happy that he was preoccupied with sending a message to Hoyt and Agent Anderson, giving her a moment to process her thoughts. She'd been silently berating herself for the past hour. Why had she told him so much about her attack? Most of her brothers didn't even know about the severity of her injuries. If she could have children or not wasn't anyone's business but her own. And yet, she'd practically told Sawyer. Oh well, that should be all it took to keep him from getting too close, making it easier for her to deny the attraction.

"There. I've updated them to our whereabouts and sent a picture of the last piece of the map." He smiled at her as he reached back with one hand and slid the satellite phone into the side pocket of his backpack. "Now, we need to think about how we'll proceed once we get close to the cabin. We can't just rush in. We have to get a visual on Kayla and Lovelorn."

"You really don't know what this guy looks like?" Bridget had wanted to ask this question ever since she'd first heard about Lovelorn, but somehow the moment never seemed right. Now they didn't seem to have anything but time. Well, at least until they made it to the location of the big red X marked on the map. In the meantime, they steadily worked their way deeper into the Appalachian Mountains.

"No. He's a chameleon. We've caught him on video several times—his back always to the camera—and each time his build and hair color were different. It's pretty easy to change your appearance these days with a box of dye and a padded bodysuit."

Another fallen tree lay in their path. The long way was definitely the path less traveled. She reached out to steady herself on the log as she lifted a leg to crawl over, but Sawyer caught her hand and pointed toward a plant covered in a dusting of snow. "Don't touch that. It's poison ivy."

"Good to know. Thanks." She moved her hand to an ivy-free spot and crossed the log. "So, how do you know the killer has been the same guy every time? Could some of the murders have been copycats?"

"There were two copycat murders, minus the poems. We caught that guy rather quickly because he left prints. He also left both bodies in a shed in an alley behind his apartment complex. Something Lovelorn has never done is use the same location twice." He cupped her elbow and guided her to the left.

He stood still. "Listen."

Bridget did as instructed. The sound of moving water drifted up to her from below. "Sounds like we're getting close to the stream."

A nod was his only response. Sawyer led the way down the slight incline. And she followed, gingerly, one step at a time, biting the inside of her cheek to keep from crying out in pain. She couldn't let him know she'd injured her ankle in the fall. If he knew, he'd insist on slowing the pace, and she couldn't be the reason they didn't make it to Kayla in time.

"Okay, so Lovelorn is a chameleon," Bridget continued once they reached level ground. "And, obviously, he's a person who holds a grudge. I mean, he waited over a year and a half to exact his revenge, and during that time, you pretty much disappeared. Correct me if I'm wrong, but it seems like only a few people knew where you were. Lovelorn would have had to track you down and then figure out the setup of the ranch to pull this whole thing off. Not to mention laying out this elaborate scavenger hunt. So, he has probably been hanging around Barton Creek for the past few months waiting for his opportunity."

"That pretty much sums it up."

How could he be so blasé about this? A jittery, unsettled feeling built inside her with each step she took closer to the mark.

"Okay, then, why don't we think about any new people who've moved to the area. Even a quick-change artist would've had to take on one persona to hang around Barton Creek. The advantage of living in a small town is that strangers stick out like a sore thumb, so it's not likely he'd have come through town multiple times dressed as different people."

"That's a valid point. The only problem is I've kept to myself. I couldn't tell you who was new in town and who wasn't."

"Really? Why?" She held up a hand, even though his back was to her and he couldn't see her. "Never mind. We don't have time for that. Besides, I shouldn't be so nosy."

Bridget nibbled on her lower lip. "Before I returned to the ranch to do my physical therapy, Grams liked to send me monthly letters the size of small novels, updating me about everything that happened in Barton Creek. She said there's a new second-grade schoolteacher. Ms. Hawthorn. She's dating the sheriff's brother. I guess we can rule her out… unless… Could Lovelorn be a woman?"

"Could be, but not likely. Mary Kate, the only victim we know of who escaped Lovelorn, couldn't identify him because he wore a disguise over his face. But she said his voice was deep, and he had masculine hands with hairy knuckles. She was certain he was male."

"Okay, let me think… Grams said there was a new ranch hand at Stone Bridge Farm. He was a former navy officer. Had an anchor tattoo on his forearm. Oh, but wait, shortly after I arrived, she told me he left town after getting fired."

"What did he get fired for?"

"He was passed out drunk in one of the ranch trucks. Claimed he was framed, but Mr. Walsh has zero tolerance for drinking, especially since his son was killed by a drunk driver."

A deep, throaty laugh erupted from Sawyer. "I never would have suspected Marie to be such a gossip."

"She's not a gossip." Bridget bristled.

He arched an eyebrow. "What would you call it, then?"

"I'd call it a grandmother trying to keep her granddaughter connected to the community where she spent her summers growing up."

"I guess."

They reached the stream, and Bridget was relieved to see that Sawyer had been correct. The water levels were low, offering them a narrow, snow-covered trail to follow.

What had Sawyer's childhood been like?

She knew he was raised in a single-parent household, making him fiercely independent.

"You never told me. What's your mom like?" The question popped out before Bridget knew what she was saying.

Silence hung in the air.

She had about given up on an answer when Sawyer's husky voice broke the silence. "My mom died when I was nineteen. She was murdered one night after leaving her waitressing job at an all-night diner."

"Sawyer…" What could she say? "I'm sorry."

"Yeah. Me, too." He shrugged, a frown on his face. "No mom should ever have to work two jobs to provide for a child she was left to raise alone, through no fault of her own."

The conversation drifted off, and they walked in silence.

Four hours later, the sun had sunk low in the sky, and shadows danced in and out of the trees bordering the stream. Even though they'd only taken two short water breaks since they started following the stream, Sawyer didn't look the slightest bit tired.

Bridget, exhausted and hungry, dearly desired a moment to sit and rest. "How much farther until we can take a break?"

"We've crossed two trails, so we should be getting close to the last one."

"The one that leads to the cabin?"

"Yes. We'll stop as soon as we get to that point, okay?"

"Do I have a choice?" She puffed air to blow a strand of hair out of her eyes.

"You're doing great." He continued to look ahead, his back ramrod straight. "As soon as we stop, I need to check for messages from Hoyt or Agent Anderson. Maybe they found Jonathan. I also want to know the location of all the agents. I know Anderson hopes to move into place to assist us when we get closer." Sawyer was talking uncharacteristically fast. Nerves? "Of course, they can't get too close or Lovelorn will see them. And it will jeopardize the entire mission."

"How will they know when to move in?" she queried.

"The button on the side of the radio that looks like a mute button is really a panic button. When pressed, an SOS signal will be sent to Anderson's phone."

"Sounds like you've planned for every scenario."

"Impossible. Okay, time to switch on our headlamps." Sawyer pointed. "I think that's our trail. We're getting closer. Be extra diligent looking for traps."

He stepped onto a large boulder and reached out his hand to her. "We'll cross the stream here. Hopefully, the sun warmed these rocks enough to melt the ice and snow off of them. But there could still be a few slippery spots, so be careful. I'd prefer not having to fish you out of icy waters twice in one day."

"No more than I'd prefer not getting soaked again." She followed him, stepping from rock to rock in his footsteps.

Once they made it safely to the other bank, they stayed close to the rocky mountainside. Eventually the path they were on intersected a more defined one. They had found the trail that led to Kayla. It was obvious this route had seen many travelers. Bridget could only hope they didn't run into any other hikers. Too many innocent lives had already been taken. She had no desire for others to be put in jeopardy.

"Okay, let's take a break. If my calculations are correct, we're about an hour and a half from Kayla. We'll sit and rest a few minutes and eat a protein bar." Sawyer led her to a log that lay a few feet off the path.

As they approached the log, an anguished moan broke the silence. Sawyer dropped his backpack and pulled his pistol out of its holster. Holding one hand out to Bridget, indicating she should stay back, he crept forward. Using the toe of his shoe, he flipped over a long sheet of bark.

What they'd thought was a log turned out to be a battered man.

Even though the man had a black eye and a busted lip, Sawyer had no difficulty identifying him as Jonathan Smith, his sister's fiancé. Sliding the gun back into place and pulling his shirt loose from his waistband to conceal the weapon, he knelt beside the victim and placed his index and middle finger just under the man's jaw. Slow and steady pulse.

Sawyer wasn't a trained medic, but he knew basic first aid. He opened Jonathan's shirt to check for other injuries and paused briefly when he felt a device that seemed like a pacemaker implanted under the man's skin. Did Jonathan have a heart condition?

"Is he okay?" Bridget shrugged out of her pack and knelt beside Sawyer. "Is he Jonathan?"

"I think so. He's pretty banged up." Sawyer patted the man's pockets. Finding a wallet, he flipped it open. "Here's his driver's license." Jonathan Edward Smith.

The man's shirt and jeans were torn and muddy. Besides the cuts and scrapes on his face, there were scratches on his hands, and one leg turned unnaturally to the side.

Sawyer nodded toward the leg. "Looks like he may have a broken leg. Let's see if we can splint it. Then we'll try to get some food and water in him. It's safe to assume he's been here at least two days. He has to be dehydrated."

They found a couple of small limbs, and Sawyer cut them to the right length to extend from midthigh to ankle while Bridget ripped a T-shirt into strips for ties.

Bridget asked, "Should we rip the pant leg away so we can look at the leg?"

"I don't think so. If he had a gash that needed attention, his pant leg would be saturated in blood, and it's not. The thick material of the denim will also act as a buffer between the tree limb and his skin." He met her gaze. "Ready?"

She nodded. Sawyer slid his hands under the man's thigh, easing the leg off the ground the slightest bit. Bridget slid the sections of torn cloth under the leg. The man stirred and grunted in pain as she placed the last piece under the knee area.

Once all the strips of cloth were in place,

Sawyer grasped Jonathan's calf and straightened his leg. Jonathan's eyes jerked open, then closed again, his head dropping back. He'd passed out. Sawyer could only imagine the pain the man was in and the horrors he'd experienced the past few days.

Bridget tied the last knot. The leg was secure.

Sawyer made his way to the backpacks and pulled out the satellite phone and slid it into his back pocket. He'd have to contact Anderson. The paramedics needed to transport Jonathan to safety.

"Jonathan's mumbling. I think he's coming around. Maybe we should try to get him to drink some water." Bridget spoke from behind him.

Sawyer grabbed the water and a protein bar and turned to face this amazing woman who had been unfazed at treating the injured man and who had yet again displayed a strength beyond anything he could have hoped for. He handed her the items and then, before he could analyze his actions, reached out and stroked her hair. She brought out his most protective instincts. When they made it out of here—he refused to think anything else was a possibility—he'd have to take time to examine what that meant.

"You take the food and water," he said. "I'll be right back."

She glanced pointedly at the phone in his pocket. He nodded. Bridget flashed a smile, then turned and went back to the patient.

Sawyer couldn't contain his own smile as he went in search of a spot far enough away to be private, yet close enough to keep an eye on Bridget and the wounded man.

The call was brief. Hoyt and the rescue team were two and a half hours behind them. The exact same number of hours until the deadline to reach Kayla and save her from being one of Lovelorn's victims.

There was nothing Sawyer could do, except try to make Jonathan comfortable and let him know the rescue team was on their way. He slipped the phone into Bridget's pack, then went to join her and the injured man.

Somehow, Bridget had gotten Jonathan into a semi-seated position. "How's the patient?"

"Physically, stable. He ate half the protein bar and drank some water."

Sawyer knelt beside the man. "I don't guess this was the way you intended to meet your future brother-in-law." He extended his hand. "I'm Sawyer."

Jonathan turned weary eyes on him, ignoring the outstretched hand.

"I know you've been through a difficult time, Jonathan, but could you tell me what happened?"

"Sawyer, I don't think he'll be able to answer your questions."

Jonathan coughed, and Sawyer watched as Bridget lifted the bottle of water to his lips. Sawyer knew she'd think he was insensitive for pushing an injured man so hard, but Kayla's time was running out. He couldn't give up now. "How long have you been here? When was the last time you saw Kayla? Can you ID the person who did this to you?"

Jonathan turned toward Sawyer, his brown eyes cold and blank in the lamplight. "Who's Kayla? And why are you calling me Jonathan?"

Sawyer snapped his gaze to Bridget. She met his eyes, then looked back at the injured man. "That's what I was trying to tell you. It seems he has amnesia."

THIRTEEN

"Two and a half hours?" Bridget darted a glance over her shoulder, her headlamp casting a glow over the area. Kayla's fiancé slept under a tree, far enough away that their conversation wouldn't disturb him.

After Jonathan had eaten, she had placed a rolled-up sleeping bag behind his head and made him as comfortable as she could.

Lowering her voice, she turned back to Sawyer. "We can't leave him here. Alone."

"We don't have a choice. Look, he'll be fine. Lovelorn isn't likely to come back now, not when we're so close to Kayla. Besides, Jonathan's sleeping, and help is on the way."

"He's immobile. If I'm not mistaken, that was a pacemaker you found earlier. What if the stress of the situation triggers a heart attack?"

"What do you expect me to do, Bridget? My sister's being held prisoner by a madman who's counting down the minutes until he kills her." Sawyer raked his hand through his hair. "Am I supposed to get this close and give up?"

"Of course not. No one expects that."

"Then what do you suggest?"

"You go. Save Kayla. I'll stay here with Jonathan."

"Leave you with an injured man who doesn't even know his own name? What if I'm wrong and Lovelorn shows up? I can't leave you here unprotected."

Bridget didn't even try to hide the eye roll, though in the darkness that surrounded them, she was sure he hadn't seen her gesture of frustration.

"I saw that."

She bit her lip. "In case you've forgotten, I'm a trained bodyguard. I'm capable of guarding an injured man. And myself. Besides, two hours—" she picked up Sawyer's wrist and checked the time "—and twenty minutes isn't that long to wait for reinforcement." *In the woods, after dark, alone?*

Dark woods had always spooked her, even more so after she'd been attacked. She could do this. She had to do this. Protect herself and the injured man from wild animals and other things that go bump in the night.

"No. Absolutely not. I can't let you stay."

"Let me?" Indignant anger washed over Bridget. *Breathe.* She closed her eyes and counted to ten. Learning to control her tongue would always be a struggle. She'd been defensive for so long. *Don't rant. Think first. Then speak. Just breathe.* "You're wasting time. I know you think it'll take about an hour and a half to reach Kayla's location, but you don't know what you'll find once you get there. Lovelorn's been putting obstacles in our path this entire time. Do you really think you won't face any when you get to Kayla?"

"There'll be hurdles. That's another reason I need you with me, to watch my back."

She would love nothing more than to *watch his back.* With her shoulder and ankle hurting from the fall over the waterfall, she'd be more of a hindrance than a help. Sawyer would be faster without her. She had to make him see that staying behind and taking care of Jonathan would be her contribution.

"I've slowed you down this entire time." Pulling her hand free, she ticked off her transgressions. "Bear trap. Rockslide. Waterfall."

He captured her hand again and pulled it to his chest. His thumb moved in slow, caressing circles as he held tight. "None of those things were your fault. All traps set by Lovelorn."

She tilted her head and looked at the face of his wristwatch again. "Two hours and sixteen minutes."

"You're a stubborn woman, you know that?"

"So I've been told." She smiled, desperate to portray a confidence she didn't feel. Bridget was sure she was doing the right thing, but that didn't make the decision any easier.

Sawyer stroked her face. "I'm going... I don't like leaving you here."

"I know. But you have to save Kayla. And I can't leave someone injured, and alone, in the woods."

Sliding his hand into her hair, he grasped the back of her neck and lowered his head. Sawyer claimed her lips in a kiss that felt like—goodbye? She put her hands around his waist and surrendered to his strength, and her fear.

He pulled back, touched his forehead to hers and whispered, "Don't let your guard down. The phone is in your pack. If anything happens, send a message to Deputy Director Williams."

She blinked away the tears as she watched him grab his pack off the ground and hurry down the trail. Sawyer didn't know yet, but she'd slipped the satellite phone into his backpack while he questioned Jonathan to see if he had any memories at all.

Bridget couldn't send Sawyer to face a killer without some form of communication. He'd be angry when he found the phone. Too bad.

Going back to where the wounded man lay, Bridget sat with her back to a tree and pulled her knees up. This position gave her a good view of both ends of the trail. No one would sneak up on her unless they came over the mountain behind her. Considering the face of the mountain went straight up, they'd only manage that feat if they rappelled down from the top.

Jonathan coughed and moaned. "Water."

Her backpack rested against the side of the tree, so Bridget twisted to reach for the canteen. She felt a tug on her ankle, and when she jerked around, she found herself facing the barrel of her own gun.

"Do you have any idea how hard it's been to lie here and pretend to be out of it while I waited for your boyfriend to get far enough away that he couldn't hear your scream?" Jonathan sneered.

Waves of shock rippled through her body and her chest tightened. "Lovelorn," she choked.

"That's what they call me." He smirked.

"Your injury?"

"What injury? I'm double jointed. I manipulated my leg. If either of you incompetent imbeciles had taken the time to look, you would have realized it wasn't broken." He laughed, grabbed her shirt collar and stood, pulling her to her feet. The makeshift splint lay on the ground. "I guess I should thank you for distracting Agent Eldridge. While he was busy telling you goodbye, I was able to loosen the splint without anyone noticing."

"What about the black eye and busted lip?"

"Compliments of Kayla. Made me mad until I realized she helped me out with my cover. Besides, I win in the long run. Kayla and her dear brother are about to die. My only regret is Agent Eldridge won't get to see my next masterpiece. Of course, I never intended for him to see you as a bride." He leaned in close, the gun never wavering.

"I'm still not sure what went wrong on that mountainside. The explosion should have killed him. And honestly, what was he thinking letting you climb that tree? I thought he was more of a gentleman than that. You didn't bruise your face when you fell, did you?" He searched her face. "You know, you're not my normal type, but I believe you're going to be the most beautiful work of art I've ever created. Maybe, after I find Mary Kate and finally get her out of my system, all my future brides will be petite redheads. Like you. I apologize for not noticing how pretty you were the day we met." He ran the barrel of the gun down the side of her face, and she bit the inside of her cheek to keep from saying what she thought of him.

Jonathan was truly irrational. She had to control her tongue, or she would push him further over the edge. Wait...

"The day we met?" She scrutinized his face, looked beyond the swelling and bruises. Realization dawned.

He rocked back on his heels, a wide grin on his face. "Ah. I see it in your eyes. You finally figured it out."

"You were parked on the side of the road outside the gates of the ranch about two weeks ago. I asked if you were having car trouble, but you said you had stopped to check your GPS. You were meeting a Realtor and had taken a wrong turn. Then a couple of days later—" She gasped. He'd been at the Maryville Diner when she'd stopped for lunch after physical therapy, hoping to see Isabella. She'd talked to another server, Isabella's roommate, who'd told her Isabella worked the night shift with Tuesdays and every other Saturday off. Bridget had planned to go back one evening, but never made it.

"That's right. I'd been hanging out in the diner off and on for weeks. I figured it was a good place to scope out women." He sneered. "I had narrowed my choice down to two. You made the final decision for me. When you told that other server to let Isabella know you stopped by, I knew she had to be my calling card to Agent Eldridge."

The implication of his words washed over her and tears of anger welled in her eyes, begging for release. She fought with every ounce of her being to keep her emotions in check. If she lost control, she'd be a goner.

"Ah, good girl. I knew you were tough. Stay with me a little longer. We'll get around to what I have planned for you. Except that'll have to wait a few more hours. First, we need to get close enough to watch your boyfriend go *boom*."

Hoyt and his team were on their way. If Bridget could keep Lovelorn talking and get his mind off his mission, maybe she could slow him down enough to give the rescuers a chance to reach them. "Where are you taking me?"

"We're going to follow your boyfriend.

Don't worry, we won't get too close." He snagged the headlamp off her head. "We'll be at a higher elevation. Now walk."

She did as he ordered. Picking her way along the dark, rocky path. "Why a higher elevation?"

"To see the fireworks."

Would he share more information if she acted like she didn't know what he meant? Or would he get angry? Only one way to find out. "It's not the Fourth of July."

"It's much better. This is the day Agent Sawyer Eldridge exits the world."

Bridget stumbled and fell forward, hitting her knee on a rock. Jonathan poked her in the back with the barrel of the pistol. "Get up. And watch where you're going. We don't want you getting hurt, do we? If you bruise your face, you'll blemish my masterpiece, and that won't do."

"If you hadn't taken my headlamp, I might be able to see where I'm going."

"Ah, then I wouldn't be able to see, now, would I?"

She turned, hands on hips, and huffed. "I'm the one in the lead. My body blocks the light so the area isn't illuminated."

"Too bad. I'm keeping the headlamp. And I'm staying in the back so I can keep this gun trained on you."

"If you shoot me, you'll mess up your masterpiece. We can't have that, can we?" There went her mouth again, trying to get her in trouble.

"The only part I care about is the face. I can shoot you in the heart." He waved the gun. "No more back talk from you. I've had all the insolence I'll tolerate. I can take you out now, won't bother me at all. It's not like I haven't already had to change my whole method anyway just to get that lousy agent." Poking her in the side, he added, "Now, move. And keep your mouth shut."

Bridget blew out a breath and trudged up the trail. Careful to keep her back to the madman, she fidgeted with her ring. Her independence wouldn't save her. Time to stop being so stubborn. Slipping a fingernail under the stone, she activated the switch that might save her life. She only hoped she hadn't waited too long.

Sawyer arrived at the edge of a small clearing with a tree house in the middle of it. Bridget had been right. Traveling solo, he'd shaved twenty minutes off his estimated time of arrival.

The stars and the crescent moon were exceptionally bright now that there were fewer trees blocking them from view. He turned off his headlamp and stood in the shadows to observe his surroundings. From his position, he could see two sides of the structure that was built suspended in air between four trees. On one side were fifteen to twenty steps that led to the wraparound deck. The tree house itself appeared to be the size of a one-room cabin with wood-plank siding. This was a good thing, since there wouldn't be many places for Lovelorn to hide.

Sawyer slipped his pack off and dug for the binoculars. His hand closed around something plastic and boxy. It couldn't be. Pulling the object out of the pack, his suspicions were confirmed.

That sneaky little redhead.

He would have a talk with her later about risks—the ones worth taking and ones that should be avoided.

Turning the phone on, he quickly muted all sounds. There were two messages, one text and one voice mail. The text from Hoyt stated that he and the rescue team had taken the shortest route, only to be waylaid by trees and boulders from a rockslide that seemed too massive to have been a natural occurrence. Because of Bridget's impulsiveness, she wouldn't have any way of knowing help had been delayed.

He replied to Hoyt, telling him Bridget had stayed behind with the injured man and to get to her ASAP.

The desire to be in two places at once was a new experience for Sawyer. He felt torn in two. Why had he allowed Bridget to convince him to leave her behind?

Sawyer did the only thing he could. He prayed. *Protect her, Lord, please.* Peace washed over him. He hadn't left her alone. God was with her. Sawyer would save Kayla, and then he'd rush back to Bridget's side.

Lifting the phone to his ear, he listened to the voice message from Agent Anderson. Ryan had spent the time since the third clue was found pinpointing the exact location of the cabin and had traced its ownership to a vacation rental company. The cabin, which was advertised as a place to "get away from it all," was only accessible by ATV. Anderson and another agent, along with Ryan and his business partner, Lincoln Jameson, were on their way. They planned to get as close as they dared and wait for Sawyer's signal.

Maybe Bridget's impulsive decision to send the satellite phone with him would prove beneficial. Once the team arrived, he could send one of the agents to help her and Jonathan. They would get to her hours ahead of the other team, and Sawyer would be able to relax knowing she was protected.

Time to assess the situation and make sure the grounds were secure before the team arrived. He couldn't have any of them walking into a trap, or put Kayla in more danger. Holding the binoculars to his eyes, he scanned the area.

The curtains were open at every window, but Sawyer couldn't detect movement. He needed to move closer.

He slipped the strap of the binoculars around his neck, then slid the phone into his pocket and checked to make sure his gun was secure. Then he darted across the field, taking the most direct route and staying low.

Careful not to make a sound, Sawyer inched up the stairs and peered through the window. As he had suspected, the first floor was one room. Along one side was a small kitchen. To the left of the kitchen area were stairs leading to a loft. On the other side of the room were a sofa, dining table and two chairs. Kayla was strapped to one chair, a single floor lamp positioned to shine on her like a dim spotlight.

Then he noticed several cylinders on the

table with wires that attached to Kayla. A digital clock counted down the time. It took a few seconds for his brain to process the scene before him. A bomb, set to detonate in fifty-seven minutes, was strapped to his sister. He sucked in air and scanned the room, his heart pounding against his rib cage. No sign of movement.

Releasing the breath, he lifted his hand to push open the window. That's when he saw the beam of blue light that shot from one side of the casement to the other. Dropping his hand, he pulled up the binoculars and zoomed in on the window on the opposite side of the room. Wires ran down the paneling and trailed across the floor to the bomb. He zoomed in on Kayla, allowing a sigh of relief to escape when he saw her chest move.

Thank You, God. She's alive. Now, please help me keep her that way.

He continued his scan of the room. The front door and the window beside it were also wired. He would have to go to the other side of the cabin to get a good look at the window where he stood, but he knew it would be wired the same way.

Sawyer worked his way around the perimeter. With each new discovery, his chest became heavier, every breath of air infused with dread. The only positive was that there was no sign of Lovelorn. Only that created an entirely new worry, since it meant the killer could be out in the woods, closing in on Bridget.

No. Focus. Save Kayla, then get to Bridget as quickly as possible.

He brought the binoculars to his eyes, while simultaneously pulling his phone out of his pocket and pushing the speed-dial button.

"Anderson."

"No sign of Lovelorn. There's a bomb strapped to my sister. Time remaining, fifty-three minutes, fourteen seconds. All the doors and windows are wired to trigger the bomb."

He heard muffled voices as the agent relayed the information. "Eldridge, Ryan Vincent is trained in disabling bombs. He's convinced he'll be able to talk one of us through the process."

"Sir, if this is a vacation rental, there could be other cabins nearby. We need to—"

"Already taken care of. The closest cabin to you is a quarter of a mile away. Ryan's on the phone with the local police department right now. They will evacuate everyone. Hang tight until we arrive. ETA six minutes, or less."

Sawyer needed to let Kayla know he was there and help was on the way. He could flash his headlamp. But if she startled, would she trigger the bomb? He worked his way back around the building to the window closest to her. Maybe she could hear him.

"Kayla, can you hear me?"

Her head snapped in his direction, and he was met with hazel eyes, much like his own. "Sawyer! I heard movement. I prayed it was you." Her voice cracked. "I was afraid it was him."

"Kayla, listen. Help is on the way. I'm sorry that you had to go through this. He used you to get to me. I promise to get you out of there."

Tears rolled down her face. "I was so happy. We were going to be married. And—"

She thought Jonathan was dead. At least Sawyer could give her that hope to hang on to.

"Oh, honey, you still can. Jonathan's safe. Bridget and I found him. He has a broken leg, but other than that he's fine. Bridget's taking care of him until we can get you out of here."

She blanched. "No! Oh, no! Sawyer, he'll kill her. He said he was going to kill Bridget after he watched us blow up."

The roar of motors rent the stillness of the night.

Sawyer yelled, "Calm down, Kayla. It'll be okay. Bridget's a professional bodyguard.

She'll be able to protect herself and Jonathan if Lovelorn shows up."

Was he trying to convince Kayla or himself?

"Sawyer, you don't understand." The engines stilled. "Jonathan *is* Lovelorn."

"What?" His heart skipped several beats, and he forgot how to breathe.

"Bridget's in trouble," Ryan shouted as he and the other men pounded up the stairs to the tree house. His arm in a sling did nothing to detract from his authoritative presence.

"Sheriff Rice called," Agent Anderson added. "Seems he's been trying to figure out why Jonathan looked so familiar. He remembered giving directions to a lost motorist about three months ago late at night on the road that leads to Mountain Shadow Ranch. Said the guy had pulled off the road about a quarter of a mile from the entrance to the ranch. That motorist was Jonathan. Then the sheriff showed the photo to his deputies, and one remembered seeing Jonathan last week in a diner in Maryville, the same diner where Isabella worked."

Ryan leaned in toward Sawyer, holding eye contact. "You left Bridget with a serial killer. You've got three minutes to brief me on the bomb, then I want you out of here. I'll get your sister to safety. I expect you to do the same for mine."

FOURTEEN

Please, Lord, spare Kayla and Bridget. I love them, and I can't imagine my life without both of them in it.

Sawyer's heart squeezed as that truth hit him. He loved Bridget. Everything about her. From her fiery temper, to her tenacious, never-give-up attitude. The way she talked ninety to nothing when she was excited. Her devotion to family. But, most of all, he loved the way she trusted him to keep her safe.

He would never forgive himself if anything happened to her.

Determination flooded him. He had turned his sister over to the Lord and Ryan, trusting they would save her. He couldn't do more. His hands fisted at his side. Time to stop a killer.

As he rushed through the dark, overgrown woods, climbing over logs and scrambling up the rugged mountain terrain with Lincoln Jameson, Sawyer sent up a quick prayer of thanks that Agent Anderson had spent the last two days gathering supplies and preparing for this moment. The NODs, night observance devices, he had brought were the best government money could buy. Even though everything was washed in green hues, the clarity was spectacular, making it easier to see where to step.

"So, Ryan's done this before? Disarmed a bomb? He knows what he's doing, right?" Sawyer grilled Lincoln.

"I know it's hard to leave your sister behind." The security specialist jumped across a fallen log, then turned in his direction. "Ryan's got this."

Lincoln's commanding air instilled confidence, which Sawyer appreciated, because at the moment he needed the reassurance that Ryan was the best.

"I pray you're right."

Lincoln stopped and checked his watch. He pushed a couple of buttons and zoomed in on the tiny screen. "One thing about Ryan, he won't abandon Kayla. If she blows up, he blows up. And Ryan isn't ready to leave this world yet. Not until he sees the man who killed my sister—his fiancée—behind bars."

Sawyer processed Linc's words. He knew

the burning desire to bring a killer to justice. Especially, one who harmed a loved one.

The night goggles made the trek easier than the headlamp had, and they quickly reached a Y in the trail. When Sawyer turned right, Linc directed him left.

They fell into a rhythm. Linc would consult his watch and point, and that's the way they would go. After several turns, Sawyer asked, "How do you know where Lovelorn has taken Bridget?"

"Did you notice the emerald ring Bridget wears?"

"Square-shaped, mounted at a forty-five-degree angle, fancy scroll design? Looks old. I was worried about her wearing it out here, but she said she never takes it off."

"That's the one."

He heard the smile in Linc's voice, and his curiosity was piqued. "It's important because…"

"It was a gift from Ryan for her last birthday. He had the ring specially designed after she was attacked. There's a tiny tracking device set in the filigree—or as you called it, fancy scroll design."

This was unexpected news. Why hadn't Bridget mentioned the tracker? "Does Bridget know she's being tracked?"

"She knows. There's a switch to turn the tracking on or off. It automatically sends a signal to me and Ryan, along with coordinates to her location. It lets us know she's in trouble. She's refused to use it, until now. Bridget activated it fifteen minutes after you left her. We knew she wouldn't willingly leave an injured man. What we didn't know until moments before we reached you and Kayla was that Jonathan is Lovelorn."

Sawyer couldn't believe he'd led Bridget, like a lamb to slaughter, into Lovelorn's trap.

Linc's watch vibrated. "They're just over this ridge."

"He's getting into place to watch the explosion." Sawyer reached up and turned on his earpiece. From this point on, it would be their only communication. "You go left. I'll go right. Wait for my signal to move in. Oh. And, Linc. Lovelorn is mine."

With his heart pounding in his ears, Sawyer moved silently through the night. Whatever it took, he would save the woman he loved.

Bridget and Jonathan reached the top of a ridge. Shadows loomed in the darkness. She struggled to make out the shapes of trees and boulders as she fought to keep her panic at bay.

"Five minutes. The fireworks begin in five minutes." Lovelorn bounced on the balls of his feet as he forced Bridget's hands behind her back and tied them with a strip of the T-shirt she'd used to secure his splint earlier.

Excitement radiated from Lovelorn. His eyes sparkled like a child's on Christmas morning.

The taste of bile rose in her throat, and she gagged, on the verge of being violently ill. If only she hadn't snuck the satellite phone into Sawyer's pack, maybe she could have sent a warning to Deputy Director Williams. A bomb squad could have gotten to Kayla and Sawyer in time. Even as she had the thought, she knew how ridiculous it was. They were in the middle of the Appalachian Mountains. A bomb squad wouldn't reach them in time.

Lord, please save Kayla and Sawyer. They need a chance to know what it's like to be siblings.

"By my estimate, your boyfriend should have gotten to his sister about fifteen minutes ago. Since the bomb hasn't detonated, he must have realized my genius. The whole place is wired to blow if a single window or door is opened." A triumphant laugh burst from the killer. "Imagine the agony he must have felt the moment he realized he couldn't get to his sister without making the whole place go *boom*.

"Get comfy. Watch the show. Too bad we couldn't get close enough to see and hear the panic. At least we'll see the flames." More triumphant laughter assaulted Bridget as he pushed her down onto the ground.

She landed hard. Rocks dug into her palms, and tears of pain stung her eyes. *Think, Bridget.* There was no way to know how long it would take help to arrive. She had to fight back or die.

Feeling the ground, she searched for something—anything—she could use as a weapon. Her fingers connected with a flat rock the size of a postcard with rough edges. Could she use it to rip the material that held her captive?

Under cover of darkness, she struggled with the rock. She lost her grip, and it clattered to the ground.

"What was that?" Her captor circled her as he peered into the surrounding darkness.

"Could be a wild animal." *Change the subject. Keep him talking.* "Isn't it past time for your fireworks? Maybe Sawyer deactivated your explosives."

"Impossible. A psychoanalysis profiling special agent couldn't possibly have the skill set needed to deactivate my bomb." He pulled out his phone. The display screen had big red numbers counting down. "Here we go. Seven... Six... Five... Four... Three... Two... One... No! Why didn't it go off?"

A flap of fabric brushed against her palm. She closed her fingers around one end of the soft cotton and tugged. Hearing the faint sound of ripping material, she shouted, "I guess that stuffy old psyc—"

"Shut up! He can't outsmart me. Doesn't he know I'm smarter than him?" The madman muttered under his breath, becoming more agitated with each word. "I will always be a step ahead," he snickered. "That's why I left a second bomb under the cabin that I could detonate from here." He pushed a series of buttons on his phone.

A remote detonator. Time was up. She held tight to the flap of fabric and rocked her wrist. With each movement, the T-shirt fabric loosened. There, she was free.

His finger suspended in air over the screen. "I'll show him."

She fisted a handful of gravel and dirt.

"Watch closely," he singsonged.

"No! You watch." She jumped to her feet. Lovelorn turned toward her, and his eyes widened. She threw the dirt at him. He stepped back, flung his arms up to block his face and stumbled. The phone fell out of his hand and clattered to the ground. Landing facedown. The earth shook as a cloud of smoke mushroomed into the sky above the trees.

A raw, guttural cry ripped from Bridget. Kayla and Sawyer were dead. She'd detonated the bomb.

"All safe and accounted for." Relief surged through Sawyer as Ryan's voice came over his headset mere seconds after the explosion. "Now save my sister."

With no time to celebrate Kayla's rescue, Sawyer sent up a quick prayer of thanks. Now it was time to save the woman he loved.

"Go! Get Bridget," he shouted into his headset to Linc.

Sawyer stepped out of the bushes where he'd been hidden, his gun pointed at the man who had attempted to take everything from him. In his peripheral vision, he saw Linc grab Bridget and drag her toward a large boulder. Her wails tore at Sawyer's heart, and he willed himself not to look at her. Knowing if he took his eyes off Lovelorn, the killer would have the upper hand.

"Agent Eldridge…" Shock registered on the

murderer's face as he scrambled backward. "How? No! You're supposed to be dead."

"Jonathan Edward Smith, you're under arrest for the kidnapping and attempted murder of Kayla Eldrid—"

"What do you mean, attempted? I saw the cabin blow up," Lovelorn scoffed.

"So it did. But you didn't get the girl." Sawyer heard the gloating in his voice. Not very professional, but he didn't care. "As I was saying—"

"My dear Agent Eldridge, you don't think I would have come into battle without planning for every scenario, do you?" Snide laughter erupted from the killer as he leaned back against a tree, crossed his ankles and put his hands into his pockets. "Give me more credit than that."

Sawyer's grip tightened on his gun. He would not let this man kill again. "Put your hands up. I. Will. Shoot. You."

"Go ahead. Shoot. And this entire mountain will blow sky-high." Jonathan lifted his chin defiantly. "I'm prepared to die. Are you?"

Even though he sounded nonchalant, in the green glow of the NODs, Sawyer could read fear in the killer's eyes. Was that a bead of sweat rolling down his face? And if it was, did it prove there was or wasn't a bomb planted nearby? He felt Linc watching and waiting.

Never taking his eyes off Lovelorn, Sawyer gave a slight jerk of his head, signaling Linc to move Bridget to safety. He didn't have to look to know Linc read his message loud and clear. Over his headset, Sawyer could hear Bridget murmur in protest. "We can't leave him. No. I won't—"

The sound ended abruptly. He imagined the bodyguard clamping his hand over the woman's overactive mouth.

Thankful for the darkness masking their movement, he waited. His gun pointed, unwavering. Time ticked by.

"If what you say is true, tell me how much dynamite and where it's hidden."

"Like I'd tell you that."

"How do you plan to activate the explosives?"

"A detonator, of course. Could be a timer or remote trigger. I'll let you try to figure out which."

Had his voice faltered? Or was that imagined? Were there explosives planted or not? Was the killer playing another game with him?

"Hoyt's team is almost to your location. ETA ten minutes," Agent Anderson's voice sounded in his ear. "Buy as much time as you can."

He was a profiler, not a negotiator. *Help me, Lord.* "What are your demands?"

"A helicopter to get me off this mountain, and safe passage to Morocco."

The killer had done his research, choosing a country without an extradition agreement with the United States. Yeah, right. Like that was going to happen. "If you wanted to go to Morocco, why didn't you go when you had the chance? You knew we all thought you were dead. Why didn't you go then?"

"Because *you* had to die." Jonathan shook his head. "I can't believe Mary Kate got away from me. It took four years to find where she ran and hid the first time. Then she escaped, again."

Surely Sawyer hadn't heard that correctly. Mary Kate had been in hiding less than two years, not four. And as far as he knew, there hadn't been an attempt on her life recently. "A second time?"

"The day she left me at the altar, and—" Jonathan pressed his lips together.

The day she escaped your attack.

Although the Bureau always investigated the men in each victim's life, Sawyer had never found a connection between Lovelorn and any of his victims. All the victims had seemed to be random women who fit the killer's preferred type, making it hard to pinpoint his next victim. So, Sawyer had had no reason to think Mary Kate had been anything more than a random target, until now.

Mary Kate had jilted Jonathan on their wedding day. She hadn't been just another random victim. She'd been the ultimate target, the person whose rejection had most likely triggered Lovelorn's murderous streak.

"You were engaged to Mary Kate. Six years ago? How long did you wait after she jilted you before you murdered your first victim?"

Jonathan sobered. "Enough stalling. You need to get that chopper in here. Now!"

"If there *are* explosives on this mountain, they wouldn't be on a timer because this would be plan B, which means you wouldn't have a way of knowing what time the bomb needed to explode."

"Nicely done, Agent. But that still leaves a remote detonator."

"Ah, but thanks to Bridget, you no longer have your remote detonator. So, would you like to try again to convince me why I shouldn't take you out right this minute?"

"Because the detonator is implanted under

my skin. A tiny device that will activate if I'm shot." The killer smiled triumphantly. "You felt it when you examined me earlier for injuries, remember?"

The pacemaker? That couldn't be a detonator. Could it?

Jonathan pinned him with an unblinking gaze. His chest rose and fell rapidly. Several seconds passed.

"What will it be, Agent? Do we walk away to fight another day, or do we both go out in body bags?"

"We're in place, sir," Hoyt's voice sounded in Sawyer's ear. "We move in on your signal."

Despite the cool temps, beads of sweat dotted the killer's hairline, and a single drop slid down his temple. Relief washed over Sawyer. Lovelorn was lying.

Keeping his voice measured, Sawyer gave the command. "Now!"

He took a step toward the killer. "Jonathan Edward Smith, you're under arrest for the Lovelorn murders, kidnapping and attempted murder."

Jonathan straightened, shifted from foot to foot, looked left, then right, then left again. Sawyer tightened his grip on his gun, anticipating the move. The killer darted right, and Sawyer squeezed the trigger.

Lovelorn grasped his upper left thigh and dropped to the ground. Before he had even hit the surface, Hoyt and another agent flanked him, gripping his arms and forcing his hands behind his back.

Sawyer waited until the serial killer was cuffed and seated on the ground. He knelt beside the man who had put him through so much turmoil. The medic who had accompanied Hoyt's team rushed over, wearing a red MediTac backpack. Sawyer locked eyes with Jonathan and lifted his hand to halt the medic from coming closer.

"Jonathan Edward Smith, you have the right to..." Ignoring all comments and protest from his prisoner and knowing another officer would repeat the process prior to interrogation, Sawyer didn't stop until he'd finished reciting the Miranda rights. The weight of the past two years lifted, and he felt like he could breathe again. Could live again.

He stood so the medic could tend the wound. Lincoln joined him. "Nice shot. But how did you know he was lying about the device implanted in him?"

Sawyer let out a puff of air and shrugged. "He wasn't lying. When Bridget and I checked his injuries earlier, I noticed a small object that appeared to be consistent with the size, shape and location of a pacemaker. I was going to ask Kayla about it and probe my *future brother-in-law's* family's medical history." He knew Anderson was listening in on the headset, so he added, "Anderson, have the doctor do a thorough examination. I want to know what the device is, a pacemaker or a detonator. Though I doubt it's possible, if it is a detonator, find out what we have to do to get it permanently deactivated."

"Copy that" came the clipped response.

Linc shook his head. "You still shot him, knowing there was a device? Were you that sure the mountain wouldn't explode?"

"I was that sure of my shooting, and my ability to read people. I knew if I grazed him with the bullet, probabilities were good that the device wouldn't detonate. Although Lovelorn likes to inflict pain on others, he wouldn't want to suffer. I couldn't imagine him taking the chance that the bomb wouldn't take him out quickly. So if there is a detonator, it would only detonate if he was dead."

The medic put away his supplies, and the two agents helped Jonathan to his feet. "I underestimated you, Agent. When you disappeared and went to work on a ranch in the middle of nowhere, I thought you had lost your edge."

The comment didn't require an answer, so Sawyer stood in silence.

"I just have one question for you, Agent Eldridge. How are you any different from me? You were willing to kill innocent people to take me out."

"All the agents here know that dying is a possibility in this line of work. We do what we have to, to keep the public safe from monsters like you."

"But what about your girlfriend?" Jonathan sneered and looked past Sawyer. "You were willing to blow her to smithereens if it meant getting me." The killer's taunting chuckle echoed as Hoyt dragged him away.

Shame settled like concrete in the pit of Sawyer's stomach. He knew what he would find before he even turned around, but he did anyway. Bridget sat leaning against the boulder, watching him as a medic attended her scrapes and bruises.

I could have killed her with my actions. Dear God, am I a monster, too?

"Don't let him get to you." Linc clapped him on the shoulder. "If you decide not to go back to the Bureau and don't want to be a rancher, let me know. I'd be more than happy to hire you to work for Protective Instincts."

Sawyer closed his eyes. "I thought you got her to safety. What if—"

"Look, man. There's no point in worrying about *what-ifs*. One look at her determined face was all it took for me to realize that trying to get her out of here would have been like wrestling a lion. So, I muted my mic and told her if she so much as sneezed before I gave her the all clear, I'd make sure that she only worked with our most difficult clients for the next thirty years."

Sawyer stared at Lincoln, his mouth agape.

The security specialist shrugged. "I knew you wouldn't do what you had to if you were worried about Bridget."

"Am I that transparent?" Sawyer asked.

Lincoln smiled and walked away, whistling. There was no answer needed. Sawyer could only hope Bridget hadn't picked up on his feelings. He didn't want to scare her off before he had the chance to sit down with her and tell her himself. But before he could do that, he had to make sure Kayla was okay.

FIFTEEN

Too restless to sit, Sawyer leaned against the wall with his arms folded across his chest and watched Kayla sleep. She looked so young lying against the stark white hospital sheet, her face battered and bruised. He could only imagine what she'd had to endure while held captive by Lovelorn.

The doctor said she would need to stay in the hospital for a couple of days for observation. She was being given IV fluids for dehydration.

Pinching the bridge of his nose, he willed his emotions to still.

Would Kayla ever forgive him for bringing a serial killer into her life? He prayed she could, but he knew forgiveness was hard sometimes. His mom's refusal to forgive his dad for walking out on them had caused her to block any form of communication between him and Sawyer.

Then once he was an adult, Sawyer's own determination to hang on to the grudge his mother had carried had kept him from ever knowing his dad, resulting in too many lost years with his sister. Of course, it wasn't until years after his mother had passed that Sawyer had learned his father had regretted walking out on him, but his mom had denied his father contact with him, keeping them from having a relationship.

A shiver ran up his spine as he recalled finding the letters addressed to him from his father. They'd been in a shoebox under his mother's bed. Sawyer had found them when he was packing up her things after the funeral, but he hadn't read them then. Instead, he'd allowed anger and hurt from the recent loss of his mother—the only person who had ever loved him unconditionally—to control him. So, he packed the letters away, thinking he'd read them someday, when his emotions weren't so raw.

That day hadn't come until nine years later, after his sister knocked on his door and turned his world upside down. Their father had died six months earlier from cancer, and he had made her promise to find her brother and try to have a relationship with him. She'd convinced Sawyer to read the letters and look at the other side of the situation. When he did—later that night, alone in his apartment—he'd read remorse in his father's words. The first letters were an admission of guilt for turning his back on Sawyer when the marriage deteriorated. Followed by a request to work together to build a foundation of trust and love. And eventually, acceptance that Sawyer wouldn't be part of his life, with an invitation to reach out at any point in the future.

"You look about a hundred years old." Kayla's voice was faint.

"Thanks, sis." He pushed off the wall and walked to her bedside. "I *feel* ancient." Sawyer searched her face, happy that she was awake and he could finally apologize. "How do you feel?"

"Grateful." She squeezed his hand. "Thank you for finding me."

Sawyer's throat constricted. He tried to swallow the emotions that welled up inside him. "I'm so sorry, Kayla. I never meant—"

"Don't you dare apologize. What happened to me wasn't your fault."

"How can you say that?"

She shrugged. "Because it's true. I'm the one who let Jonathan into my life. I fell for his lies—"

"That's not your fault. He targeted you."

Sawyer knew victims often took the blame for things that happened to them. He refused to let his sister believe she was responsible for what she'd been through.

"Yeah. I know. Jonathan is a sick man. But it still remains that he couldn't have orchestrated all of this if I hadn't fallen for his lies and let him into my life." She offered Sawyer a sad smile.

No point arguing with her now. However, with a master's degree in psychology, he knew she had a long road of recovery ahead. He'd see that Kayla had excellent counselors to help her overcome this trauma with minimal effects.

"I'm sorry I've not been there for you. I love you." Bending, he kissed her forehead. "I promise to be the best brother from here on out."

She wrapped her arms around his neck and pulled him into a hug. "I love you, too, Sawyer. And I'm very thankful to have a big brother who's the best FBI agent ever."

There was a knock on the door. Sawyer straightened as Agent Anderson walked into the room. "Ah. I see our patient is awake. Do you feel like answering a few questions?"

"Do you mind if I stay?" Sawyer asked.

"Fine with me if it's okay with your sister."

Kayla nodded consent, so he went back to his previous spot on the wall and listened quietly.

Twenty minutes later, when the questions began to focus more on his sister's romantic relationship with the killer, Sawyer pushed off the wall and cleared his throat. "Time for me to excuse myself."

He kissed Kayla's forehead and headed for the door. As he passed Anderson, he whispered, "Be gentle. She's been through a lot."

The older agent clapped him on the shoulder. "I know."

With a nod, he stepped out into the hall. Torn between staying nearby or looking for Bridget, he paced the length of the small corridor.

His third time past the nurses' station, he sighed and turned to the nurse who had checked Kayla's vitals earlier. "Ma'am, when Agent Anderson leaves, could you please let my sister know I had to go somewhere, but I'll be back soon?"

Before she could utter a reply, he was sprinting down the hall. He had to see Bridget, and he couldn't wait a moment longer.

Bridget sat in a private waiting room with a view that overlooked the city of Knoxville watching streaks of orange and red paint the sky as she tried to tune out the noises of the hospital staff and FBI agents bustling around in the corridor. This was the fourth sunrise she'd witnessed in as many days, and with it came a peace like she'd never known before.

Lord, thank You for letting me live to see this beautiful sunrise. I pray Sawyer will allow You to give him the same peace that You've given me.

She'd spent the last few months running from the words of the doctor who'd told her she'd never bear a child. She thought she'd accepted that she was damaged and could never love or be loved. Too bad her heart hadn't cooperated.

Bridget loved Sawyer.

She'd known she was attracted to him from the moment she stepped on her grandparents' ranch two months earlier, but the sheer strength of her love for him had barreled down on Bridget when she'd thought he'd died in the explosion. Then he'd faced Lovelorn, and he'd been unwavering. His protectiveness and courage amazed her.

The gray vinyl chair squeaked, and she glanced over to see that Ryan had sat down beside her.

"Hey, Pe—" He sighed. "Bridget."

She smiled and laid her head on her big brother's uninjured shoulder. "It's okay, Ryan. You can call me Peanut or Munchkin or anything else you'd like. I realized something out on the trail the past few days."

"What's that, Peanunchkin?"

She giggled, and he smiled and winked.

"I love you, Ryan. I'm very blessed to have you as one of my big brothers."

He held his chest, pretending to be wounded. "It took you two days in the wilderness to figure that out?"

Bridget giggled. "No, I've known that I love you for a very long time. What I figured out in the wilderness is that no amount of wishing or running will change who I am. So, I might as well embrace all the things that make me…me. There is good in every flaw, even those that seem wretched and impossible to overcome."

Ryan—the only person other than her parents to know the depth of Bridget's injuries—put his arm around her and hugged her tight. "I love you, you know that?"

"I know."

Ryan had never been one to use words to express his feelings. He showed his love to his family in many ways, like dropping his pursuit of the man he'd been chasing around the world for four years to come home and save her from a serial killer.

Sawyer walked into the waiting area, and hesitated in the doorway.

"Looks like someone else wants to talk to you," Ryan murmured. "Guess I'll go see if there's anything I can help Hoyt with."

Heading toward the door, Ryan threw one last look over his shoulder. "Oh, and try to stay out of trouble for a while, okay, Peanunchkin?"

Sawyer raised an eyebrow in her direction. Bridget smiled and shook her head. Any other day she'd be mad at her brother for sticking her with a nickname she knew she'd never live down, but not today. Today, she had too much to be thankful for.

Stepping into the doorway and blocking Ryan's exit, Sawyer said, "Before you go, I was wondering what you thought about the device implanted in Jonathan's chest. Could it be a detonator?"

"Anything is possible. Of course, it would require having a doctor implant the device. But, if he could pull that off…" Ryan shrugged. "With the right program, and having the heart act as the countdown clock, who knows? I would imagine it'd only work in close proximity to the bomb. Since the mountain didn't blow up when he was taken into custody and removed from the location, I'd say either the detonator is just a pacemaker and nothing more, or he didn't have a chance to sync the devices."

"Thanks, Ryan. Guess I'm going to have to be patient a little longer and see what the doctors say. Oh, and thanks again for saving my kid sister."

"Don't mention it. You saved mine. Makes us even." They clapped each other on the back and bumped shoulders in a move Bridget liked to call the "man hug."

Bridget struggled to tamp down the beginnings of a grin. "Hey, I was doing perfectly fine on my own."

Ryan looked back through the door and caught her eye. "Perfectly fine at detonating bombs." He winked, then strode down the hall whistling "Fly Me to the Moon."

Sawyer stared after Ryan, shook his head, then entered the waiting area. "Peanunchkin?"

A few short hours ago, she'd been afraid of never seeing this man again. Joy washed over her, and her heart did a happy dance in her chest. "A new nickname. I have a feeling this one will be harder to shake. But you know, I don't think I'm going to mind."

"You guys have such a close, loving relationship. I wonder if Kayla and I will ever have that or if half siblings just can't be that close."

"Sawyer, Ryan and I aren't biological siblings. Mom and Dad adopted him when I was five. He was ten."

Shock registered on his face. "I never would have guessed."

"It's not something we go around talking about, but we don't try to hide it, either. I'm only telling you so you can understand it doesn't matter if you share one parent, two parents or no parents. Blood isn't what makes a family. Love is."

Love makes a family. Even if a child is adopted and doesn't share your DNA, love makes him yours. Her heart smiled. *Message received, Lord.*

"Oh." He slumped in the chair Ryan had vacated, exhaustion carved on his features. "I wasn't sure if you'd still be here. I thought you might have gone back to the ranch to be with your family. I'm sure your parents and siblings have arrived for Thanksgiving."

"They have. I'll be heading to my grandparents' soon to see everyone. After all, this year I have a lot to give thanks for. Surviving two attempts on my life, among other things."

Like falling in love with you. "Will you join us at the ranch tomorrow for Thanksgiving?"

"I'd like to, but I hate to leave Kayla."

"Then I'll just have to bring you both some leftovers."

A smile spread across his face. "That sounds good. Do you think you might have one of the ranch hands bring me a change of clothes before then? I'd like to shower."

"Definitely." Bridget's hand went to her hair. She felt grubby. Except for the unexpected dip in an icy plunge pool, she hadn't bathed in days. She must look awful.

Although, how she looked was a minor issue. The most important thing was that she and Sawyer had survived Lovelorn's game of death. Compared to that, nothing else mattered. The only thing that could top it would be if Sawyer cared for her the way she did him.

Sawyer caught her hand and laced his fingers with hers as he silently berated himself for mentioning his desire for a shower. Her hand had instantly gone to her hair. He wanted to tell her she was the most beautiful woman he'd ever seen, and no amount of dirt or grime would change that. But he knew she'd laugh his words off and not believe him.

Time to change the subject. "Anderson allowed me to sit in while he questioned Kayla about Jonathan."

"Did you get any answers?"

"Yeah. It seems he was very chatty, especially the week he held her captive leading up to the last four days. I guess he figured she wouldn't live to tell anyone, so there wasn't any harm in venting to her."

"Did you find out how the dead professor was connected to Jonathan and how Agent Miller's body ended up in the trunk of his car?"

"Jonathan told Kayla the professor was his father. He planted the dead body to frame him because he left Jonathan and his mom when Jonathan was a toddler and never acknowledged him as his child. The Bureau will conduct DNA tests to corroborate the story." Sawyer leaned his head back against the wall, closed his eyes and sighed. "It's strange to think that our childhoods were similar. You know, in all the years that I've worked as a profiler with the Bureau, the possibility that I might have something in common with any of the killers never once crossed my mind."

She squeezed his hand. "A *similar* background is where the commonality stops. It just proves where we start out in life does not have to define the rest of our lives. Each person has free will to choose the path they take and shouldn't blame the outcome on circumstances."

"I agree." He sighed.

"So, how's Kayla?"

"According to the doctor, she's going to be okay. The physical scars will heal, but the emotional scars will take longer."

"She may even have to learn to live with some scars that never completely heal," Bridget surmised.

"Yes." He frowned. "It's hard seeing someone you love struggling and not be able to do anything to fix it."

"Tell me about it. When Jonathan was threatening to blow up the mountain, and I had to watch you in a standoff with him, knowing you were a sacrificial man who would do anything to protect innocent people. And you could die before I could tell you I love you. I thought—" A look of shock crossed her face, and she faltered.

"I hoped, but didn't dare dream, that you could." A smile split his face. "You love me."

Her face beamed, and his heart soared. Then, just as quickly, the joy in her eyes shuttered, and he knew she was overthinking things again. He couldn't allow her to do that. Even if she hadn't meant what she said, if it had been a slip of the tongue, he had to tell her what she meant to him. Love was a gift and should never be kept secret. "Bridget, I—"

"Before you say anything, you need to know that my scars run deep." Bridget's voice quavered. "You know about the attack that almost cost me my life. You've seen the scars. What you don't know is the wounds to my abdomen caused damage that will affect me as long as I live."

His phone rang, and he bit back an exasperated exclamation. Deputy Director Williams's number flashed on the screen. "I'm sorry. I have to take this. I'll be right back." Sliding his finger across the screen, he put the phone to his ear and crossed to the window. "Agent Eldridge speaking."

"Sawyer, I just got off the phone with the attending physician who is overseeing Jonathan Smith's care. It's been verified that the object he claimed was a detonator is indeed a pacemaker. It seems Mr. Smith was born with a congenital heart defect that contributed to him needing a pacemaker installed his junior year of college eight years ago."

Sawyer puffed out his breath. "Thank you for letting me know."

"You made the right decision out there. I hope you realize how much we need you in the Bureau."

"Thank you, sir, but I don't know. This still doesn't change—"

"That's enough. For such a smart man, you can be very obtuse sometimes. You were not responsible for what happened to Vicki. She is the one who decided to follow a lead on her own without backup. And no one in the Bureau, myself included, holds you responsible. I know you think your colleagues distanced themselves from you after the incident, but in reality, you were the one who pulled back. Not the other way around. I tried to tell you this before, but you wouldn't listen." A sigh came across the line. "I had hoped the time away would have helped you put things into perspective. Guess I was wrong."

Sawyer turned to look at Bridget. She sat silently watching him from across the room. He really needed to get back to her and finish their conversation before she changed her mind. "Sir, I hear what you're saying. I promise to give the matter a lot of thought and have an answer for you by the end of next week."

Disconnecting the call, he returned to the seat next to Bridget. But before he could speak, she placed the tips of her fingers against his lips.

"Please, let me finish before you say anything." She offered him a wobbly smile. "You need to hear this. So you can decide if a relationship with me is worth the sacrifice. Because of the damage…and the scar tissue… The doctors told me I have less than a ten percent chance of ever conceiving a child."

With the utterance of the last word, Bridget looked down at their hands, clasped tightly. Sawyer's heart drummed in his ears, as he waited for any indication he could speak now. Several long moments later, she lifted her tear-streaked face and met his eyes.

Sawyer pulled her hand to his lips. "May I speak now?"

She nodded.

Sawyer cupped her face with his free hand and brushed her tears away with his thumb. "Sweetheart, having you in my life will never be a sacrifice. Besides, didn't you just tell me *blood doesn't make a family, love does*? As far as children are concerned, we'll have to wait and see how many we're blessed with, biologically or through adoption or both. I trust God to handle that. After all, He sent me you."

"But, Sawyer, I have so many flaws. Some

of them I'm working on—like talking too much. But some of them, I have no control over. I know I come across as an extroverted, bubbly person, but deep down inside I'm a terrified introvert who's afraid of being judged and misunderstood by others."

"Ah, sweetheart. I know you have flaws. Remember, I'm the guy who spent two days in the wilderness with you. Hey!" He ducked to miss her playful swipe. "I love your quirkiness." He kissed her forehead. "I hate to break it to you. I'm not perfect, either. But I promise you one thing. If we—two imperfect people—work to build a loving relationship, it may be the most perfect thing we ever do."

Sawyer bent and brushed a kiss across her lips. "I love you, Bridget. And I promise to remind you of that fact multiple times every day."

Bridget rewarded him with the brightest smile he'd ever seen. "I love you, too."

His heart swelled. Lowering his head, he claimed her lips in a kiss full of love and promise.

EPILOGUE

Bridget sat on the bank at the edge of the waterfall that was located on the side of the Appalachian Mountains that bordered her grandparents' ranch. Sawyer had suggested a picnic at the waterfall she'd fallen off of six months earlier. But she hadn't been ready to relive that hike, even though that experience had taught her it was impossible to outrun fears because they would always follow you around until they were dealt with once and for all.

She sighed. Where was Sawyer? She craned her neck and searched. His note had instructed her to be here at noon on the dot and warned, if she was late, he wouldn't share his big news. Bridget hoped his news meant he'd made a decision about his future with the Bureau. His leave of absence had ended two months after capturing Lovelorn. Since then he'd been working with Special Agent Anderson out of the Knoxville office. But Deputy Director

Williams wanted him back at Quantico, and Sawyer was supposed to make his decision this week.

"I see you're on time, for once."

Sawyer came through the trees wearing crisp, dark jeans, a white button-down shirt and his black Stetson on his head. He carried a wicker picnic basket with his left hand, a plaid blanket thrown over his arm, and he held a bouquet of wildflowers and roses in his right hand.

"Of course I was on time. I didn't want to miss your big news." She turned her face upward as he bent at the waist and received his kiss. "Mmm. Hello, handsome."

"Hello." Another kiss. "Sorry I kept you waiting. I had to make one last phone call before I left the office."

He offered her the flowers, and she buried her face in them, inhaling the sweetness of their fragrance. "Thank you. They're beautiful. But what are we celebrating?"

"Life. Love. God's perfect timing." He set down the picnic basket and spread the blanket on the ground.

She stood to help, but he halted her. "No. You sit right here. I've got this." He started unloading the contents of the basket: fried chicken, potato salad, rolls, cheesecake. "Tell me about your day. Will the office be ready to open on time?"

"Yes." She smiled. "Protective Instincts' Knoxville office will open as scheduled. I hired a secretary today, and Linc flew in to interview the team of bodyguards."

"Linc? I thought Ryan planned to do that."

"He got a lead on Troy so—"

"He flew off chasing him." Sawyer shook his head. "I wish he'd let me help him. I'm sure—"

"Honey, I know you want to help him catch Troy, but this is something Ryan has to do for himself. I think chasing Troy has been very cathartic for him. Even though Ryan was a marine and had no control over being deployed, he has a lot of guilt over not being there to protect Jessica. Being the one to track down Troy Odom is his way of making it up to her. I'm sure he'll ask for your help if he feels like he needs it."

"I guess you're right."

"Enough about Ryan." She patted the blanket beside her. "Sit down. Tell me. What's your news? Did you decide to go back to Quantico? Or are you going to work out of the Knoxville office? Or become a full-time ranch hand? Or maybe join the circus?"

He sat beside her and pulled her into his arms. "Now, how could I possibly join the circus and spend all my time traveling the world without you? Unless, of course, you want to join the circus, too, and then I'd have no choice but to follow you."

A giggle bubbled up inside her. "You'd do that?"

"Without a second's hesitation." He hugged her tighter. "This feels nice."

She snuggled in close. "I think I'll skip the circus life. We'd be too busy walking tight-ropes and taming lions to take time to enjoy moments like this."

"I agree." He kissed the top of her head. "You have a way of messing up a man's plans, did you know that? I had this entire after-noon planned, down to the last detail. But why should today be any different? You bar-reled into my life, a little pixie dynamo who talks ninety to nothing, with an infectious laugh and a smile that outshines the sun."

Releasing her, he sat up straighter, slipped a hand into his pocket and pulled out a key. "I bought Stone Bridge Farm today." Bridget squealed and threw herself into his arms as he continued. "I couldn't imagine living so far away from you, so I turned down the offer to teach at Quantico. I'm going to be a full-time rancher, but I have agreed to be a consultant for the Bureau on important cases."

"I'm so happy." Bridget kissed his face.

Firm hands on her shoulders gently pushed her back. "There's more." He shook his head and laughed. "Why do I ever try to plan anything with you?"

Giving him her wide-eyed innocent look, she said, "I don't know what you're talking about. But if you're going to learn to be spontaneous, can we throw away all your notepads and lists?"

Her sassiness was rewarded with a firm but all-too-short kiss.

"No. But if you'll let me continue, I'd like to finish what I started."

Bridget rocked back to her original seated position. "Okay. I'm all ears."

If, as he'd said, her smile could outshine the sun, the one he gave her at that moment was in a whole other universe.

"When I came to Barton Creek, I was running from my failures and couldn't imagine ever feeling at peace. Now, I know I'm a simple man with simple needs. With the purchase of Stone Bridge, I now have one of life's most basic needs…a home." He slipped his hand back into his pocket, and her heart skipped a beat. "But the most important thing I need in this life to make me happy and complete…is you, by my side. Always."

He opened the black velvet box that he'd pulled out of his pocket, and her breath caught. It was the most beautiful ring she'd ever seen. A brilliant oval-cut diamond, mounted horizontally in an antique platinum setting. "Bridget Vincent, I love you. Will you marry me?"

Tears streamed down her face as she nodded.

"Is that a yes?" He laughed. "Are you actually speechless?"

She exhaled the breath she'd been holding. "Yes. Yes. Yes! Of course I'll marry you." She didn't know how he got the ring onto her shaking hand, but he did. And a flood of emotions and excitement washed over her. "I can't believe you planned all this. Everything's so perfect. And I'm so happy. How soon ca—"

Sawyer's lips claimed hers, silencing her. He pulled back and smiled down at her, his eyes twinkling. "Is that the only way to make you stop talking?"

Bridget giggled. "If that's the punishment, I'll talk even more."

Sawyer laughed and claimed her lips once again.

Thank You, Lord, for seeing me through the storm and blessing me with this man.

* * * * *

*If you liked this story from Rhonda Starnes,
check out her previous
Love Inspired Suspense books:*

Rocky Mountain Revenge
Perilous Wilderness Escape

*Available now from
Love Inspired Suspense!*

*Find more great reads at
www.LoveInspired.com.*

Dear Reader,

Thank you for reading *Tracked Through the Mountains*. I'm thankful this story of redemption and love has finally made it into your hands. I hope you enjoyed Sawyer and Bridget's love story as much as I enjoyed writing it. These characters are very near and dear to my heart. Their story has been a work in progress since 2015.

You were first introduced to Bridget Vincent in my debut novel, *Rocky Mountain Revenge*, when she helped protect the heroine's sister. I had many readers ask me to write her story next. What they didn't know was I had already written it. However, the story needed to be polished, and I needed to learn patience. Remember, all good things come to those who wait.

I would love to hear from you. Please connect with me at www.rhondastarnes.com or follow me on Facebook @authorrhondastarnes.

All my best,
Rhonda Starnes